Way of the Unfaithful

Sinmisola Ogúnyinka

The story is purely fictional and represents the craft and imagination of the author.

Any coincidence of the fictional names and places with real persons, living or dead, and real places, is unintentional.

No part of this book may be reproduced, stored in a retrieval system, or transmitted by any means, electronic, mechanical, photocopying, recording, or otherwise, without written permission from the author.

This book is licensed for your personal enjoyment only. This book may not be re-sold or given away to other people. If you would like to share this book with another person, please purchase an additional copy for each recipient. If you're reading this book and did not purchase it, or it was not purchased for your use only, then please return to your favorite retailer and purchase your own copy. Thank you for respecting the hard work of this author.

Cover Illustration: Amazingrafiks © 2017

Author photo: Cybermul © 2010

For my Christian sisters; Peace and Remi, who've been through the works... And every woman who deserves a change.

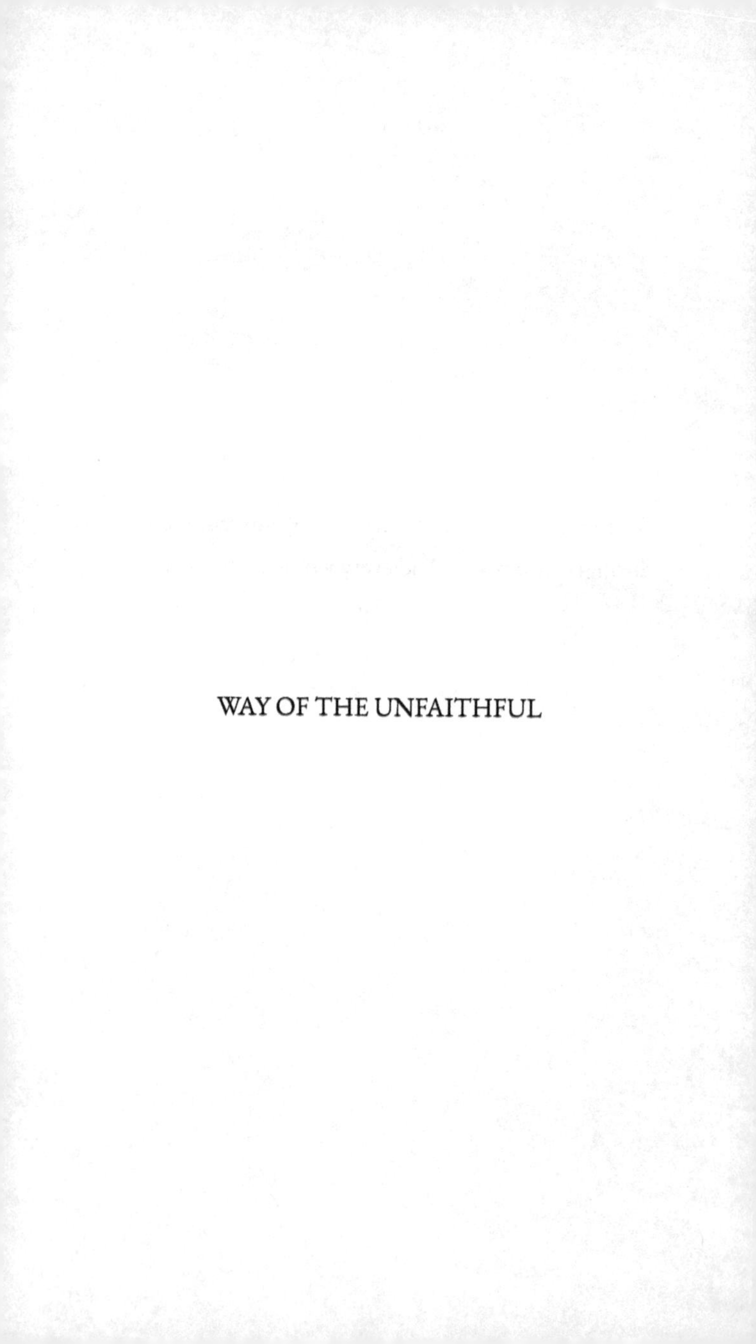

WAY OF THE UNFAITHFUL

CHAPTER-ONE

July 2007, Calabar

Kokei rolled over on to her stomach and sighed satisfactorily. Small beads of sweat earlier broken off her temple trickled to her cotton nightgown and soaked through to the silk cover of her king size bed. She rounded up her session of prayer with a wave of thanksgiving and stood, to gingerly step into her turquoise bedroom slippers. She yawned and strolled into her walk-in wardrobe to select a beige and grey floral dress.

Dodeye would soon be home with the kids and she needed to have her afternoon bath to welcome them. Hers was a made-in-heaven marriage. Her life was perfect by all standards and she was only ever grateful to God. She laid the expensive linen dress on her bed and went to the bathroom to do her facial treatments.

She always made sure she fixed her face religiously during her morning bath, her afternoon bath and her evening bath. She had started the rituals as a young, single woman and ever since remained faithful to it.

No wonder her thirty-eight year old skin remained ever firm and supple. Of course, that was mainly due to the fact that she could afford the best and most expensive treatments for her skin. Coupled with access to good food and a conducive living condition, Kokei could not have hoped for much more. Besides, she was a relatively contented woman and God had been ever so gracious to her.

Kokei Keyu was married to one of those Christians with a voice in their Calabar society. Dodeye Keyu was not only a government official with a lot of steam, he was also a highly successful businessman. Life with him had been full of excitement and positive challenges. As his wife, Kokei had been more exposed than most other women in public view. She attended functions to represent her husband and to identify with others in the same class with her. She was involved with the activities in church, and she used her talents and creativity to register her presence.

Kokei had a bachelor's degree from the University of Calabar in Marketing but went on to learn Interior

Decoration. She added finesse to her skill and produced designs in a class of their own.

Though a housewife, she worked her small but lucrative business from home and was usually busy but never enough to neglect the detail of her home and marriage. Dodeye had married a truly godly woman who gave apt attention to the welfare of her home despite outside pressures.

Kokei had barely finished fixing her face when her handsome husband walked into the house. The usual chatter of the children didn't follow him. The soft sole of his leather shoes tapped the glass tiling as he came up behind her. The face reflected in her mirror where she sat at her dressing table, applying a light blush to her checks, was grim. Something was wrong. Kokei's first premonition was for the children.

She turned to face him, her pulse raced. "Honey, you're back early. The children?"

"I dropped them off at the Henshaws'. We need to talk."

We need to talk.

Dodeye's opening remarks for war or trouble. Had she offended him? Kokei respected her husband for all the right reasons and more. More than anyone could imagine.

She only knew where she had been, where she was coming from. Not even Dodeye knew the half of it.

"What is it?" She failed as usual to hide the slight trembling of her voice. Everything had gone well in the morning before he left with the children. "How are the children?"

He pressed his lips together. "I dropped them off at Henshaws'."

The children were not due out of school till two o'clock, another ten minutes away. He must have picked them at least an hour early.

We need to talk. She looked into his beautiful eyes, as dark and deep as a well. Kokei could not read what was behind them. His angular face became passive. For a brief second, she thought she saw a jaw muscle twitch. Her fair skin tingled beneath her freshly applied make-up, and her palms became clammy.

"What's wrong then?" This time, the trembling of her voice was evident. She touched his wrist lightly. Her huge eyes searched his out under his thick black eyelashes.

He tossed a letter on top of the fine cedar wood dressing table. "Read this."

Kokei picked it and read. Dodeye walked away to the other end of the room and leaned against the wall, his gaze diverted away from her. He looked calm but the tension in the room thickened as she put the letter down and stood.

Studying him, she knew she had to choose her words. Dodeye was a docile person. Even in the midst of a storm, he always knew how to handle his emotions.

"This is strange, isn't it?"

His voice was barely audible. "It is."

Why he was disturbed, she couldn't understand. The letter spoke of no trouble. To her, there was no big deal.

She moved closer. "I wonder who could have brought the issue up."

Dodeye frowned at her and again she pondered what she must be missing. The content of the letter was strange only because she could not imagine where the contact was from. She had an idea of what the scriptures expect to be done about it.

After all, you cannot serve God and any other thing.

She stood in front of her husband and nestled her head against his broad chest. She wished she knew why he was so quiet.

"It's not something you can consider," she whispered and looked up at him. A chieftaincy title in the village? No.

He returned her gaze. "It is."

His steady look seared into the depth of her soul and she knew at once, why he seemed troubled. She had expected he would agree with her. He had known he wouldn't.

Kokei tensed against him. Was this the trouble?

Yes. She pulled away a fraction and sighed. She never used force to catch his attention or change his mind. She also learnt not to be rash in her reactions. He must have good reasons for considering this abomination in the first place.

"Maybe you should go back to work. We can talk about this after dinner." Her palms splayed out on his chest. She didn't plan to seduce him... Yet. It had worked several times.

After a good meal, a good bath, and after a good bath, a good massage, and afterward—

"I came to pick you up to the village. We see the *Obol Lopol*." He breathed in. "Today."

He spoke with conviction and a sense of duty, and this time, she withdrew from him.

The Obol Lopol -is the royal title of the king of Ugep, their hometown.

She tried to control her alarm. "The village?"

"Get ready. We need to get back today," he said with a note of finality.

She made to say more but he stopped her with a wave of his hand. He walked into the wardrobe and pulled out a clean kaftan.

Dodeye hardly wore any of his numerous native attires.

One of the elders in the village, and a close friend of the extended family had given him this black one with simple, exquisite black embroidery. Was this the work of Obol Otoma Ofem? She gaped at him too confused to move. Dodeye pulled off his shirt and tie as though in a dressing competition.

He was ready before she could bat an eye.

"I'm waiting in the car," he said, his voice so low she barely heard him. He was out of the room before she could respond.

Ugep town?

CHAPTER-TWO

October 1985, Ugep town

Kokei Kepam Leko sat in the front pew of the church with her fanatic mother on one side and her sisters, Wofai, Womi and Komommo on the other. The Reverend Father served the Holy Communion and she couldn't keep still any longer. She wondered what they were doing in church anyway. God had forsaken them. Wofai's father, the recent 'hope' for their future had walked out that morning, and Kokei couldn't believe her mother would still pack her four daughters, all from different fathers, and come to church.

Which God did they think they were?

The last time the man of the house left, it was Womi's father. He had beaten them all up and left with what little money was in the house. That was six years ago. This is better forgotten than compensated.

Those days were rough and mean and they had starved on several occasions.

For over a year, they had picked from dumps to keep body and soul together and then one day, Kokei had come home from scavenging to find

Wofai's father in their one-room accommodation. He was a burly of a man, come to think of it, all their fathers were brawny men. Her mother had described their father as a giant, and she had taken some of his height. At sixteen, she already towered above her 5'5 mother.

Wofai's father had a rough-hewn, hardened face. He looked as though he had not shaved for over a week. Surprising, his eyes were soft and smiley. His nose, wide and crooked looked like a workman's mistake. The thin nostrils were large and contorted. He had the most re-markable nose Kokei had ever seen. With the eyes of the twelve-year old, Kokei thought he was handsome.

Odd.

He was chocolate-coloured with thick, bushy hair. As she entered with a customer bag' containing her small finding, Wofai's father stood.

"Good evening, sir."

"Call me uncle. I have come to take care of you," he said, unsmiling.

Yet his funny smiley eyes, danced. Kokei felt a
ridiculous chagrin, and quickly passed through the
room to the backyard where she found her mother was
busy cooking.

Cooking!

There had been no cooking in the house for more
months than she could count. Mma looked up and
smiled, her usually creased face, lit up. She was a beautiful woman. Where she lacked in height, God made
up to her in other endowments. Despite the fact that
she had three daughters, her fair skin still looked firm
and young. Her pearl shaped eyes were well protected
by long lashes. Her hair was dark and long, thick and
curly. Her slim figure was curved in all the right places,
her bust though a bit heavy for her slight frame, was well
complemented by well-shaped and rounded hips. Kokei
had taken everything from her, except the height. And
in deference to her mother's often bushy eyebrows, hers
were slashes of black that swept upward across her, fair
and flawless, lustrous skin. "Mama, I'm back."

"*A-won-ke*," Mma greeted cheerily.

The aroma of the soup wafted to Kokei's slim,
pointed nose and she leaned closer. Vegetable
soup! She couldn't believe it. She smiled at Mma,
questioningly.

"He is a good man," Mma said, looking toward the house. Kokei also looked as though to confirm what her mother had said.

He had better be, she thought warily. Mma never revealed anything more about him.

He proved to be for four years. He gave money and visited often. Sometimes, he spent the night, sometimes Mma left with him and the girls stayed the night alone. Wofai was born shortly after he came into their lives.

One morning, three years into the relationship with Wofai barely two years old, he moved in. Kokei never really knew if he had a family or not but somehow, he was always there. Then one morning, at about 4am, she heard Wofai's father and their mother in a heated argument.

He did not hit her and he repeatedly told her to keep her voice down. And then there was silence. When they all had the courage to stand up from

their mats and see what was going on, Mma was alone, getting ready for the day.

When they looked at her questioningly, she simply shook her head.

"He's gone."

Now as Kokei sat, enduring the boring progression of religious worship she wondered for the umpteenth time why she was ever born. Her life was so miserable. She felt wretched. At sixteen, she was nothing. She had nothing. She barely existed. Her mother lived off men and that was it. She knew she would never live like her mother. She would not prostitute and still be poor.

Either prostitute and be rich, or remain poor.

"Pay attention," Mma's stern whisper came through to her.

She straightened and tried to concentrate. As long as she was under Mma, she would simply abide. The worship service closed long after Kokei came to this decision.

Steeling herself against all the thoughts on her own mind, she went out of the house as soon as they got back. She couldn't imagine what this new development could mean.

Wofai's father had stayed longer than the others. In fact, Kommomo's father had not stayed long enough for the girl to be born.

With Wofai's father, there had been some stability in their lives. The man had tried to be the father none of them had ever known. Now he was gone!

The sun had already set when Kokei got back home. Mma sat by the side of the dilapidated bungalow they shared with several other tenants, praying softly but as Kokei made to pass by, she stopped and looked at her.

"Where are you coming from?" Mma muttered.

"Isalo's house."

"She is not a good girl."

Kokei breathed noisily, and clenched her fist. Her anger apparent. "Who is?"

Mma sat straight. "You will not talk to me like that!"

For the first time, she noticed her oldest daughter. Kokei was no longer a child. The soft swell of her bosom, the slimness of her waistline and flat stomach, the round mound of her hips,

and buttocks, her long slim legs... soft, full lips, and small pointed nose, her pearl-shaped eyes, and those long lashes... Mma's face dropped to stare at Kokei's bust line. She was full. Fuller than her!

"I'm sorry, Mama but the truth is bitter." Kokei moved to leave. Mma stood abruptly. Kokei was a head taller now.

"What truth? I am your mother. I will slap you if you talk to me anyhow."

"If you touch me, Mama, I will leave you, and you will never see me again!"

Mma gasped. "What is the meaning of this?" She pulled Kokei to face her. "After all I have done for you?"

"Perhaps what you have done for me is the beginning of my problems. Why did Wofai's father leave you? All about being good?"

Mma slapped Kokei. Kokei did not touch her stung cheeks. Rather she looked down into her mother's eyes.

Mma placed a hand on her heart and stared at the cold darkness in her daughter's eyes.

Something had definitely happened to this child. Kokei, her first blood. Her defender. Kokei was really the mother of her other children. She had always watched her back. What had happened to her child?

Isalo! Isalo was a bad girl.

"If you are good with your word, Mama, I'm good with mine. It's a pity, we are so much alike," Kokei said under her breath.

"I didn't mean to slap you. What has happened to you, child?"

"I am not a child anymore!" Kokei wailed. "I grew up. That is what happened. You were busy trading yourself. That's why you never noticed." Kokei yelled.

This time, Mma had no apologies. She raised her hand to deal another slap but Kokei caught her hand in time.

"*Se na a ko loh,*" she spat and turned round, running off.

"Kokei! Kokei Leko!" Mma shouted into the night but the girl was gone.

Her knees buckled under her in sudden realization, and she crumbled to the floor. Mma hardly ever cried. She was from a tough stock. But this was too much. The first thing that happened to her was Yibala's departure, early in the morning. Yibala, Wofai's father. Warm, caring, foolish! Why wouldn't he accept that she did what she did to sustain them all?

And now Kokei! Her first child, the beginning of her strength, her might, her dignity. Gone! Run off into the night. Into the dangers of the world. She would look for her. She had to. Her other three children couldn't take care of themselves without Kokei. She burst into tears before she could control it.

CHAPTER-THREE

January 1986, Ugep town

Isalo sat with her bare legs dangling over the side of the low fence, as she chewed noisily on the local sweet pepper fruit. Her eyes were diverted away from the hot January sun high overhead. Not a cloud in the clear blue sky bothered to compete with the dominance of the sun. There was a strange calm about the town of Ugep as the masses milled around about their business as usual.

"Are you hearing me?" Kokei said, looking longingly at her friend.

She and Isalo had only recently become friendly. But within the short space of time, she had come to love and respect the other girl. For her age, Isalo was full of experience about the world, and deep understanding and sympathy. She had heard so much about Isalo that had put her off the other girl, but when fate drew them together, Kokei discovered the other girl had been grossly defamed.

"Continue," Isalo mumbled.

"Mama sleeps with anything male. Wofai's father pleaded with her to stop. Said he would go back

to the farm to sustain us.

"Mama was still bent on opening her legs everywhere!"

Isalo picked another fruit and bit into it. "She was being sincere."

"Why do you eat that thing?" Kokei said, annoyed. "I hate the smell."

Isalo shrugged. "It kills mouth odour. It is good. You should get used to eating it."

"Did you say sincere?!" Kokei returned to their conversation as though she had not interrupted it at all.

Isalo spat out the head of the pepper fruit. "Yibala is a big fool. He cannot work hard yet he wants to eat like an elephant."

"Isalo! You are so blunt! Wofai's father was the closest thing to love and care anyone had ever seen in that house"

"But he cut a chunk too big for him to chew. Call your mother a slut, whatever." She rolled her eyes. "She is still one of the most beautiful women in this town. The next twenty years, and men will still desire her."

Kokei winced. "I can't believe you are talking like this. They were just using her. She definitely wasn't living well off all those men."

Isalo snickered. "I guess she was too soft-hearted. Too many men owing her for services rendered."

Kokei looked at her fingers, shamefully. "Oh Isalo."

She hated herself for being the daughter of the 'town slut'. She hated her mother. And she hated Isalo for rubbing pepper on a fresh wound. But then, wasn't this what everyone was saying. Even the men knew they could owe. And her mother wouldn't stop "falling in love" with her customers. Always hoping he would marry her and give her a better life.

"Look Kokei, I'm sorry for being so harsh. But you are too much like your mother. If you are not careful, you'll end up like her, maybe worse. Because you are more beautiful than she is."

"I'm so confused. I'm so afraid."

"You have to be strong. Men are not worth the salt."

"What do you know about men?"

"I know enough. That's why I have vowed. They will be like toys in my hands. They will serve me, and not the other way."

"How do you hope to achieve that?" Kokei looked at her friend longingly, hopefully. As one would look upon a god!

"I'm leaving this town. Too many fool men in this town. Poverty-ridden, foolish men. All men are fools." She laughed suddenly. "I will go for the rich fools. Use them and dump them," she said. "Port-Harcourt is the greatest. Lagos is heaven!" Isalo said, her eyes widened in ecstasy.

"How did you know about all these towns?"

"My aunty lives in Calabar. She has been to Lagos once and she told me about all those other towns. For a beautiful girl like you, the sky is not wide enough!"

"We don't have education beyond primary 6. How can we relate with rich men? Isalo you dream too big!" Kokei said resignedly.

"You dream not at all. I will not live on stinking, poor men who will beg to owe me. I will not allow men like Yibala, big for nothing with eyes bigger than their privates, seeking to live a life they cannot afford, and pleasures they cannot buy.

"Men like that will not father my child." She rolled her eyes. "Please Kokei, if you want to be like your mother, go back to her."

She jumped off the wall with a thump and strolled back into the two rooms she shared with her parents, three brothers, two sisters, and now Kokei.

What other life did one have a chance at? She reminisced over her own dreams. School, a good job with the government. A decent life. A decent husband and children. She even dreamt of cleaning up the mess her mother had made of her life. Could that ever be possible with Isalo as her helpmate? Prostitution in a high class. Prostitution was prostitution. High class or low. She also jumped off the wall and walked slowly back to the rooms. Three options before her struggled for admittance. Go back to her mother. Go with Isalo wherever she was headed or take off on her own.

Kokei thought of the sweet pepper fruit. Pepperish, bitter-sweet, kills odours.

CHAPTER-FOUR

September 2007, Ugep town

Kokei recognised Obol Otoma Ofem at once even though he was dressed in the usual traditional wrapper, chieftaincy and cap all the other elders wore. He sat in the midst of several other chiefs and chatted softly. Beside him, a young woman sat. She was beaded from head to toe but beneath the beads, Kokei sited a blooming flower. She couldn't be more than twenty years old. All around her, the elders broke kolanuts and sipped gin.

Kokei recoiled. Dodeye was nowhere in sight and though this was his father's house, he had probably paid for the entertainment.

Papa sat at the far corner of the large sitting room, whispering into the ears of one of the female elders. She looked too young to be a chief. Probably in her mid-forties, or less.

Kokei couldn't say but then, in the village, chieftaincy followed a strict matrilineal or patrilineal structure and unlike in many other places, movement, dress code, and general life is restrictive, yet not rewarding in Ugep and Yakurr

generally. Kokei felt some pity for the woman who was obviously trapped by the culture.

Obol Otoma Ofem looked up as she walked in and gazed at her. There was no friendliness in the stare just a bland, empty look. She did not have a friend in this company. They were all fetish, ugly, demon-infected people. She counted eight or more chiefs, apart from the beaded girl who she assumed was Obol Otoma's latest bride, the female chief and Papa. What was she doing here?

"Kokei, come and sit down, my dear." Papa waved to her and she walked over to him, smiling warmly.

At seventy-eight, the old man was frail but still commanded respect from all who knew him. He was a kind and generous man, and though a polygamist like most men his age, especially those like him in the Obol Lopol's council, he was a man who understood her more than any other person. More than her husband.

She squatted in front of him in the traditional manner of greeting before taking a seat to his left side. She noticed the older woman speak with him, eye her for a moment before going over to take the

seat beside Obol Otoma Ofem.

Strange!

She had been subjected to all manner of strange behaviour since the first day Dodeye gave her the letter to read. The letter offering him a chieftaincy title in the village, well town Ugep was no more a village. The town had grown so much since she left it over twenty years earlier.

"Whatever happens here today my dear, take it as the good hand of fate. Don't disgrace me," Papa whispered into her ear.

His breath reeked of whiskey. Kokei cringed. Whatever would happen? She did not reply but prayed briefly under her breath. What more could happen? They had visited the village twice before today and each time, there had been gatherings like this. Only that the beaded girl had been absent previously. The meetings were held to convince Dodeye of his role in the society and the strong need for him to be in the Obol Lopol's council. Ironically, Papa had been least insistent on Dodeye taking his seat. Truthfully, the seat could be given to anyone in the family.

To Kokei's dismay, Dodeye's older cousin, who

had earlier been offered the title had politely declined and no one had bothered him.

Dodeye had also been told to decline if he wished. No, he did not decline. He did not accept either. Bad news both ways. Instead, he had subjected them to these trips, with the excuse that he wanted to know more about the whole idea. What on earth for?

Dodeye walked in, clad in a grey guinea voile chieftaincy shirt and black trousers, with black snakeskin leather slippers. Kokei had never seen him in the traditional attire before. When she had been summoned into the meeting, there had been no one to enquire her husband's whereabouts from. She was a total stranger in this family. Despite having been married to them for over ten years, they still treated her with deference.

Though Dodeye built his house on the outskirts of town, he insisted they stayed in the rambling ranch-style house owned by his father. The compound was large with chalets belonging to different wives, and they stayed in the main house with Papa, shunning his mother's more private quarters.

"Papa, *a wi loh.*" he squatted briefly before taking the seat to Papa's right.

"*Eiya,*" Papa mumbled.

Dodeye did not spare her a glance though she desperately stared at him in a bid to catch his attention. Where was the Bible-College-Alumnus-husband she married? Her heart rippled with fear.

Obol Otoma Ofem stood to greet. "*Mbi ya won.*"

The house chorused in response. "*Iya!*"

Kokei sat tight-lipped. Praise the Lord was more like the greeting she needed to respond to right now.

"Our fathers say the man they are bringing a wife to, need not stand on his toes. A word is enough for the wise. Our son, Dodeye Onen Keyu, is an illustrious son. He is a son we are proud of. A son we can display anywhere."

"Hmm...hmm," the other chiefs grunted.

Kokei crossed her legs nervously and then uncrossed it. Then she crossed it again.

"It is not only in the word of mouth," Obol Otoma bit into the kola in his hand with a snap, as though to lay emphasis. The chiefs made more annoying noise. "The modern market was built by

him, single-handedly." He paused for effect. "The generator in Obol Lopol's palace was bought by him." He bite into the kola again, chewing ceremoniously.

"He has given over twenty of our sons and daughters scholarship up to university level." The chiefs began clapping.

Kokei looked at her husband and he looked at her. For the first time. His stare was defiant. She blinked rapidly. She had feared all these philanthropy would one day spell trouble. Why that, she had never known. Dodeye had always been generous with his money. To her, to her children. To her family. To his church. His family. His hometown.

"We have never called him, and he refuses to do our bidding. Is there anyone here that has not received from the hands of this great son?" He looked at each man, eyeball to eyeball. No one indicated. "It is time to give back. Obandi!" He looked at the beaded girl. Kokei leaned forward. Papa tapped his foot. Dodeye clenched his teeth.

Obandi stood and came to kneel in the centre of the room, facing everyone. Kokei had a good look

at her. She was dressed as the native custom required of a precious gift. Her hair was braided into long locks and beaded at length. Her face was lightly made up mostly with dark colours.

It helped to accentuate her large eyeballs, her high cheekbones and her full lips. She had chocolate, brown, creamy complexion. She looked so young too, and pretty. She could not be more than twenty. Most probably less.

Obandi did not look at anyone but simply stared down at her fingers. A multi-coloured velvet material was secured around her chest and another with slightly conflicting colours around her waist, signifying fruitfulness. Heavy beads clamped her upper arms, and wrists. Ironically, she wore no earrings but the beads in her hair and the ones around her neck, uncountable and in varying sizes, and lengths, all pink and red, signifying royalty, more than made up for lack of jewellery on her ears.

"This is your gift, true son of the soil. We appreciate you," Obol Otoma Ofem said.

Kokei jumped up, enraged. "A gift? For what? As what?"

"Woman, be silent!" It was Papa, her strongest ally.

Kokei sank back to her seat. Hot tears burned her eyes and slopped down her cheeks. Jesus! Jesus. Jesus. She chanted beneath her breath.

"Adorn your gift if you accept her," the old man continued as though he had not been interrupted.

Dodeye brought out gold earrings from his pocket and walked to Obandi. He placed the beautiful jewel on her ears. Kokei surged forward but Papa held her back. She wanted to scream, go mad. A gift. They were marrying a second wife for her husband in her presence and had little regard for her. They had never had much regard for her, anyway. She bite hard on her lower lip. What was Dodeye doing? What was all this? She watched the progress of the ceremony through blurred vision.

"A young virgin. The son of Keyu's slave. To do as he wishes. A gift from the people of Ugep. Obandi, beloved. This is what he has named you." Obol Otoma pulled her up and with her left hand in his right and Dodeye's right hand in his left, he raised the two hands up and shouted. *"Mbi ya won!"*

"Iya!" Resounded and they burst into clapping.

Kokei jumped up and ran out of the sitting room, wailing like a child, clutching her flared skirt in her hand, her heart broken beyond repair, torn from her chest.

CHAPTER-FIVE

January 1986, Calabar

The entrance into the city of Calabar was paved all through and Kokei stared hard, heart thumping in her chest. Isalo sat calmly beside her, looking as indifferent as possible. In truth, she was as nervous as her friend and her palms and feet were moist with sweat.

There were few houses as they approached the city. The weather was dreary to match Kokei's mood. She had not been able to sleep and besides dozing a little at the start of the journey, her eyes had been wide open.

They had left Ugep in first light and barely two hours later, reached their destination - Calabar, the first federal capital of Nigeria. There wasn't much to show for it. But definitely much more than Kokei had ever seen. There were several tall buildings so high up on either side of the road as they approached the car park.

"I'm so scared, Isalo," she whispered just before the bus driver switched off the engine and asked the passengers to alight.

Isalo ignored her and got out. What they were doing was the most foolish thing Kokei could ever imagine, yet, she had come along, like a sheep to the slaughter. They had left Ugep without telling anyone except Isalo's junior sister, Avakpa. They had nothing on them. No money, no clothing. Even the transport fare had been on an arrangement made with the bus driver. Isalo had had sex with the man for three consecutive nights to pay their way! Hell...

"Come." Isalo pulled Kokei with her toward the main street. "We have to be smart. And we have to find my aunty's place."

"Do you have any money?"

"We don't need money now. When we do, we will get. That good for nothing driver can always arrange friends for us but I'm not in this town to trade in poor old fools....."

Kokei drew back. "I don't think this is a good idea. Isalo, I feel we should go back to Ugep. Let's go back home, please." She gripped her friend's hand.

"We don't have transport fare. If you want to go back, I'll introduce you to Okanke the driver.

"Two nights with an amateur like you should pay your way back," Isalo said bluntly looking into her eyes. She shivered. Isalo was impossible. "Tell me, have you been opened?" she said, and Kokei cringed. What had she found herself in? She thought warily.

"Yes," she whispered.

She felt increasingly disturbed about her decision to stay with Isalo. Only three months and now she was beginning to fear she had picked the worst of the options open to her.

"In our leisure, we should talk about it. Right now, we have to move ahead and find Obal's house. If you are coming, then let's move. If not, let me settle you before I go," Isalo said blandly. This was all business to her. She sounded so impersonal.

Kokei breathed. "I'm coming with you."

"Good."

Isalo continued on the way briskly and Kokei wondered if she knew where to go. She did not dare ask, however. If this was the fate she had chosen, she had better live with it and probably enjoy it.

The two teenagers roamed for a while before Isalo decided they should go back to the park and seek Okanke's help.

They had not been able to locate Obal. The address they held, had no house number and Obal simply was not a name anyone had heard of in the neighbourhood.

They loitered the car park for over six hours, tired, hungry and feeling more foolish than they had ever imagined, before Okanke arrived from his second trip to Ugep. He introduced them to another driver who lived in Calabar before he made the return trip back home.

Abaloke, the new driver took them to his one room accommodation, and bought bread for them. They both chewed hungrily, refusing to acknowledge their mistake. Holed up with a driver, Kokei could not begin to imagine how huge their error was.

"What next?" She asked, dusting her mouth as she washed down the dry bread with water. At least she was not hungry anymore.

Isalo snapped. "Can't you think? Must I do the thinking for you? Please leave me alone."

She sighed. "Now that we have eaten, maybe we should go and look for Obal again? What do you think?"

"I think someone must teach you how to make some money so it can start coming in both ways from tonight." Isalo hissed and stood from the bench she had been seated on.

Kokei flinched. This was such a nasty girl. Isalo walked outside and surveyed the environment. It was a high-population neighbourhood. This was the heart of town. Downtown. The slum. The area of the masses. If she knew Obal very well, she was not residing anywhere near here. She wouldn't either. She hadn't paid transportation all the way to Calabar to sell herself to the masses. She shaded her eyes and looked left and right.

The sun had been covered briefly by the clouds helping momentarily to lessen the scorch of the day. A large gutter ran through one side of the street. It was filled with stagnant water and refuse. Worse still, it stank. The whole street stank. The air was murky with stench. No, if she needed this, she would have had more than enough back home.

Kokei came up behind her, and she stiffened. "I am not as ignorant as you may think. My mother's boyfriends started taking a preference to me when I turned thirteen.

"Womi's father was the very first. They come when they know Mama has gone out. At times, they waylay me and take me to their houses." Kokei breathed in deeply.

Was she being interviewed for a job? Why was she telling Isalo all this? It had been hard enough for her to take it to thought. Why did she feel she needed to make an impression on this hardened girl? Why was Isalo so hardened? Isalo's life had been better than hers back home.

"Good for you." Isalo clenched and unclenched her fists. "You will get more experience here. I'm not all that experienced either. My father was always too impatient," she said harshly, and ducked back in.

Who?! Did she say her father? Kokei's hand went to her mouth in shock. Poor Isalo. She followed her back in and found her ransacking the room. She wanted to ask why but held her breath. She wasn't about to get in the other girl's way right now.

"No money in this damned room." Isalo cursed. "Let's go back to Obal's street. I think I saw one

fine hotel on the road." She kicked some shoes out of her way.

"Anything you say," Kokei murmured, and followed obediently.

They found the hotel and asked to see the manager. They were let into a small office with a large table and swivel chair. The curtains were drawn, making the room a bit dark despite the fluorescent light. The room somewhat stuffy. A middle-aged man with a small pot belly and thin moustache sat behind the table and looked at them with hooded eyes, studying them with narrowed eyes. Isalo was the spokeswoman.

"Good afternoon, sir. My name is Queen, and this is my friend, Giftie. We just in from Port Harcourt today to meet with our uncle but we can't find him. The address he gave us is incomplete and we don't know what to do now," she said. It took all of Kokei's acting ability to play along.

The man arched an eyebrow. "Where's the address?"

"He told us Goldie by Mount Zion. He said the house is a storey building at the junction. But there's no storey building anywhere around the

junction and when we asked around for him, on one could tell us about him," Isalo said.

"What is your uncle's name?"

"Um, Obal," Isalo stammered. She had not expected all this enquiry. What was he asking silly questions for? If he wanted to assist them would he not?

"Obal is a girl's name. You two are lying aren't you?" The man barked. They startled. "Are you prostitutes?"

"Please, sir." Kokei stepped forward. "It is true that we are stranded. We don't have anywhere to go. We don't have money to go back to Ugep. Please help us." Real tears trickled down her cheeks and Isalo scowled.

The stupid girl was messing up their chances with her crocodile tears. The man studied them carefully for a while. Ugep!

"You are from Ugep not PH!" He smirked. "I will give you two a room at the back," he said around a sigh. "You will pay me at the end of each week. Five naira a week for one room. If you need two rooms, it is ten."

Isalo gasped. "Five naira a room per week? It is too much!"

"Look here, we do not allow commercial sluts in this place. Those rooms I'm giving you is on private arrangement.

"If you don't want, get out!" He pointed to the door.

"We will take one room, sir," Kokei said quietly.

"I will show you the room. Now, you must remain out of sight as much as possible. No loitering is allowed. We have respected guests here who will not appreciate your presence here. You are very lucky to have this place so behave yourselves." He glared at them. "If anyone asks you, tell them you are guests. Children of a big man who have accommodation problem whilst trying to sit for certificate examination. Do you understand?" They nodded eagerly.

Their room was a long narrow strip, which looked more like a wide corridor partitioned and cut from a longer one.

A 4x6 bed occupied most of the space, and a small window opened beside the door. The room looked freshly painted with blue paint. The only source of light was a small blue bulb attached to the

ceiling fan. The bed rocked probably from a loose bolt. The bed was neatly made with a worn-out but clean bed cover and sheet. A lone wooden chair was placed against the wall where a full-length mirror was screwed on to the door leading to a small bathroom with shower and toilet.

Isalo yelped with joy. Water ran! What more could they ask for? Looking like heaven already. She turned to Kokei spontaneously and hugged the other girl. Five naira a week was too much but the room was good enough. They sat hunched together after the manager left, and made plans on how to earn at least eight naira a week.

This was just the beginning.

CHAPTER-SIX

Isalo brought two dresses with her and a few personal effects. Kokei had nothing of her own but had used Isalo's things ever since she left her mother. They had their bath, changed clothes and washed the ones they had worn, spreading it out on the wooden chair, and placing it under the fan to dry. They needed to work immediately or take a loan from the manager for the time being. Kokei didn't think the manager would indulge them though she was ready to try all options. As they made to leave, there was a knock on the door.

Isalo arched her eyebrows. "Who is it?"

"Room service," a male voice replied.

The two girls looked at each other. What on earth was that?

"Wait a minute," Isalo said.

She took a quick glance at herself in the mirror. "I will go and see him outside," she muttered and left.

Kokei leaned against the door and tried to listen but it was futile. She felt so nervous. She was only sixteen, but sexually, she was much older.

She had hated every experience she had with men and so, in a bid to keep herself from hurting, had done all she could to forget. But she never could forget. The memories were always as real to her as though it was all reoccurring.

Isalo came back in, her footsteps as light as feathers. Kokei had not heard movements. She had been lost in thoughts of her miserable past.

Isalo sat on the bed and pulled off her shoes. "Hmm...*na wa o!*"

"What did he say?" Kokei said, heart thudding.

"That manager wanted to know if we want him to arrange outings for us. They don't want us working here," Isalo said, her expression unreadable.

"What—how is...?" Kokei gasped. "So what did you tell him?"

"What else? We have to earn our living. So, I agreed. But I told him we were hoping to start work today since we don't have any money." She pursed her lips. "We have come on a dry day. No parties on Mondays or

Tuesdays usually. And today being Monday, we may not be able to work till Wednesday!"

"Maybe we should ask for a loan."

"He offered to give us N2 but…"

"But?"

"He wants you today and tomorrow."

"Me? Why me? You told him to take me?" Kokei cursed. "Isalo you betrayed…."

"Listen. He asked for you. I don't care why! You came to this town to be a prostitute so you'd better get it into your skull. You didn't come here to watch *Ekpe*. If there's work, you do. And N2 is generous for just 2 days' work. And mind you, my name is Queen from now on and you are Giftie." Isalo spat.

Kokei shrunk away from her and stood in front of the mirror unconsciously. Isalo laid down on the bed and closed her eyes.

Kokei studied her through the reflection on the mirror. Isalo was not a pretty girl but she had a beautiful body. Her skin was dark and she had pimples on her face.

Subconsciously, Kokei touched her own smooth, creamy skin. Fair, daunting, attractive. The manager had good eyes. But Isalo could more than make up for her less-than-pretty face. She had wits and had her way with men. Kokei was almost sure

she had volunteered her to the manager. And this hurt deeply.

"When does he want me?"

"Now! He already sent N1 as advance," Isalo said with her eyes still closed.

Kokei gasped. Her heart thumped. "Okay, I'm off then." She swallowed hard. She opened the door and turned as Isalo sat up to look at her. "Isalo, please..."

"Queen. I'm Queen, Giftie."

"Queen. Please buy bread or something before I come back. I'm already feeling hungry."

"Work hard." Isalo snickered. "You'll be famished when you come back." She winked. "But milk and bread will be ready for you."

***

Okokon, the hotel manager watched Kokei zip her skirt into place. The girl was melancholic. He had been impressed by her quiet obedience while they had sex but grossly disturbed by her demeanour afterward. She looked so young and virginal but he discovered quickly she was not the latter. He wondered why such a beautiful girl would be whoring at her age.

"Giftie," he said, staring at her as she smoothened a small tear on her skirt.

He had wanted her so much when she walked in, he had almost ripped the clothes off her back.

She continued what she was doing. He leaned forward and tapped her and she jumped, as though unaware she had company.

"*Ufan*," he said softly. She stood stiffly, staring at him like she was seeing him for the first time. "I want to help you," he said. "Sit down on that chair. Let's talk." She did. "Tell me what happened to you. How come you're here?" His voice softened. "How old are you?"

"Going on seventeen," she muttered.

She looked into his eyes and despite herself burst into tears. A few minutes earlier he had devoured her like a hungered lion. She had never been with any man who was so vicious. Isalo had probably given her to him, she thought bitterly. But why was he being kind now? Sated? Sober? Fake?

"Tell me everything," he said hoarsely.

"Isa....Queen will be waiting for me."

He shook his head. "What is her real name? What's yours? I want to help you."

"My name is Kokei Leko. We came from Ugep." She sniffed between sobs, and let out her story to a complete stranger.

"Obal? I know a few Ugep ladies who live around here. I will help you ask them," he said. When he smiled suddenly, a chill ran through her spine. "You are such a beautiful girl. Come. Come here."

He pulled her off the chair to his side and started kissing all over her face. For several seconds, she thought she would not be able to walk when he was through with her.

CHAPTER-SEVEN

*D*ecember 2007, Calabar

"Sir, *amesiere*, Aunty!"

"*Mesiere, nde. Idem fo?*"

"*Osong*. Please have your seats."

Dodeye sat in his swivel chair opposite Pastor Bassey, and his wife, Atai. The office was tastefully furnished with state of-the-art and wrought-iron chairs in the waiting area. Potted plants hung here and there and a woodwork portrait hung on one side of the wall while an oil paint portrait hung on another side. The floors and walls of the office was ceramic and glass tiles. The office table and cupboards were from choice pine wood, and the chairs Italian leather

All morning, the notorious Calabar rain had refused to let up.

"Can I get you something hot? This rain doesn't look like it will finish today." Dodeye looked from husband to wife. "Or you prefer cold drinks all the same. Ginger beer, juice? Or soft?"

"No, please," Pastor Bassey said. "We are all right."

Dodeye smiled at Atai. "Aunty, you too?"

She shook her head with a smile. "I'm fine, thank you."

Pastor clasped his hands on the table. "Bro. Dodeye, you probably know why we had to fix this meeting with you."

Dodeye leaned forward. "Yes sir."

"You are a Bible College graduate, and more importantly you are a good Christian. It cannot be mentioned in our midst that a child of God has a chieftaincy title from the village, or a second wife. We cannot serve two masters. Either we love the one and hate the other," Pastor Bassey said. "I cannot begin to tell you how shocked I was when I heard." He paused for breath.

Dodeye smirked. "Sir, I hate to interrupt but all this happened over two months ago. Why are you just coming? I didn't marry a second wife. And I haven't even taken the title. I don't know where all this is coming from."

"Your wife told us a few days ago. We were surprised that she kept it for so long," Atai said.

"Well," Dodeye sighed. "Things haven't been too smooth between my wife and me in the past

two months or thereabout.

"I know what informed your query but the information you have is not true." Dodeye tapped on the polished surface of his table.

"Can you give us a true picture of things?"

"Yes I can, and I will. Right now," he said. He chewed on the insides of his cheek for a moment, contemplating the next statement. "My father called last year and told me he would love to relinquish his seat in the Obol's council to me. The seat of Obal Nkpeli was vacant and he had been asked to bring anyone from his family." Dodeye stood, and shoved his hands into his pocket. "My father asked me but I told him no way. My Christian values stood in the way. He had asked my older cousin who was not too educated but though he declined, the Obol specifically implored my father they wanted an educated person, and especially, they wanted me because I had been so involved in the development of the town.

"What was I to do? I decided to honour my father, research into the culture of the land a little more, and give the offer a thought. And that is the current position. The Obol Lopol sent a letter of offer about four months ago but I haven't given a reply."

He shook his head. "My wife is just being paranoid."

Pastor scratched his chin. "They gave you a wife and you accepted."

"Sir, in my tradition, it is a taboo for the elders of the land to give you a gift and you reject it."

"Not like a wife, brother!"

Dodeye raised his voice. "Not a wife. A gift. I can use her for anything I want. Give her as a gift to my wife, or use her as a servant or maid or child in my house." He looked away. "Or I can decide to take her as my wife."

Pastor flew to his feet. "That's the bottom line isn't it? Anyhow you choose to *use* her, she will end up in your bed."

"Pastor," his wife whispered, touching the sleeves of his shirt.

"Pastor, I respect you. I love you and I listen to your counsel but I can't believe that you would listen to my wife and draw your conclusions without even hearing my part."

Pastor Bassey snapped. "What has that got to do with the information? Why should I credit you more than your wife?"

"Pastor, please take it easy," Atai said softly.

"So what is your point, sir?" Dodeye kept his fidgety hands in his pocket and stared at the floor. He noticed what looked like a stain and used his polished Italian leather shoe to scratch at it absentmindedly. "What exactly is wrong with a chieftaincy?" He looked up at his pastor but turned away at the pained expression on the clergy's face. "I'll really like to know anyway."

Pastor took calming breaths. "The rituals. The libation. The stigma. The curse. Brother, everything is wrong with the chieftaincy!"

Dodeye paced. "Is it right for a Christian to accept an academic honorary degree, or a national award or such things or partake in beauty pageant or a Pears Baby of the year Award or a a lottery. What can a Christian partake in exactly?"

"Brother Dodeye, please sit down. I'm sure Pastor will explain these things to you." Atai looked at her husband pleadingly. "Pastor, please be patient."

Pastor heaved. "Brother, a chieftaincy title is

not the same as these things you enumerated. A national award, an honorary degree and such things are what the Bible calls giving honour to whom honour is due.

"No strings are attached. Beauty contests and such, lottery and others, is just what I believe to be gambling.

It is unnecessary. It is more like tempting God. I don't believe in it and I don't agree to it. As for chieftaincy title, it is dabbling into the territory of the devil. Conjuring spirits, evoking the dead, entering blood covenants with evil, paying obeisance to dead gods. It is not your portion in Jesus' name."

"Giving honour to whom it is due, you say, sir. That is exactly what my people are doing right now. There will be no incantations, no libation, none of all this evoking you have talked about. Of course they will pr ay..."

"In whose name? When praying, who will they call on?"

"On whoever I want. Jesus, the name above all names," Dodeye said defensively.

Pastor screamed. "They would have done all the fetish deeds before coming to the open to face

you."

Dodeye fired back. "But how do you know that?"

"I know. I researched into some of these ceremonies and though I'm not a native of your town, the Obal Nkpeli is a senior chief and they will not reduce the standard for your sake."

"They will. They are doing everything to make me take the offer. They want educated folks in the council and they have several already. They want enlightened people and they want to modernise the culture..."

"Listen to yourself! Let me tell you the truth. If you want this thing, go ahead and take it. Take the second wife they have given you. Ruin your life, your wife's and your ministry. But remember, whoever breaks the hedge, the serpent will bite. A word is enough for the wise." Pastor Bassey stood and Atai followed suit.

Dodeye glared at them. "What about Christians who have taken these titles? You want to shield Christians from everything - politics, culture, professional association, social clubs - what? How do we reach these people if we are not among them? Even Paul said he was Jew to Jews and

Greek to Greeks."

"Did Paul break the law of God? Did he pour libation to other gods, evoke dead spirits and marry two wives?"

"No. And I am not doing any of those things either. We are not entering any shrines but really, I can't see how anything I say can convince you. And as for Obandi, I am not marrying her! She was given to me to help in convincing me to take the title. They believe she is temptation enough. Pastor..."

Dodeye perched on the edge of his table. "Please sit down and listen to me." Pastor and Atai remained standing, shaking their heads. "Obandi is a very beautiful girl. I will not mince words that she is more beautiful than my wife. And I am truly tempted.

"But the way everyone is going about this issue is simply further pushing me away, toward her. Kokei has been impossible these past few days. Do I have anyone ready to listen at all to me? I have not taken any decision yet and really I need help..."

"That is what puzzles me...that you can even give this a thought in the first place. Think about

it." Pastor clasped his hands again.

"We will not stop praying for you. You have every excuse to do what you want to do but I haven't heard you say it will bring glory to the name of God!" Pastor shrugged. "Let's pray together before we leave you."

He didn't wait for Dodeye's response. After a brief prayer for forgiveness and direction, he made to leave. Dodeye handed a bulky envelope to him but the pastor declined.

"Sir, you cannot reject your son's gift. It is not done. Though Isaac had no blessing for Esau, he still ate the food he brought and gave him some sort of blessing..."

"Brother Dodeye, you should be an ordained clergy and not an Obal Nkpeli," Pastor Bassey said and took the envelope. "Thank you. We will keep praying for you."

"Thank you very much," Atai murmured when he gave her another envelope containing a cash gift just like her husband's.

"The pleasure and blessing is mine, sir," Dodeye said.

Long after they had gone, Dodeye discovered

he still could not concentrate on anything. He decided to go home.

***

Kokei was with three other people from the church. They had prayed for several hours while Pastor was with Dodeye and were about to leave when he came in.

He greeted politely, and excused himself into the room. When Kokei came back from seeing the visitors off, she found him throwing clothes into an open travelling bag on the bed.

"You're travelling somewhere."

He didn't pause in his actions. "You know. You know all things don't you?"

"You're upset. Please," Kokei said. "Darling, talk to me."

He lowered his voice. "You do know all things."

"What have I done?"

He clapped. "First question in the past six months thereabout. The Madam Know-all finally has something she doesn't know." He hissed.

She moved closer and grabbed his arm. "Please."

"Listen to me. Pastor Bassey and his wife were in my office today, thanks to you. They didn't have much to say that was encouraging.

"But you know the irony, they helped me to make my mind. If I can't trust my wife to understand me, sure I can find solace where I need it most."

"I don't understand, honey."

"Baby, you forget I do have a *second* family in the village. The last time we were there, when she was given to me, Obandi begged me to take her. Fresh young blood. " Kokei cringed. Dodeye moved to the walk-in wardrobe. "Yeah. You don't like the sound of that 'cause you had none to offer. Tell you what, I'm taking the woman. And probably staying back to build a family and a community." He returned with a pair of leather shoes and threw into the bag. "Run to Pastor and tell him I said so. I dare you." He zipped the bag and pushed it to the floor.

He picked his briefcase, and placed it where the bag had been, opened it and leafed through some documents.

Kokei turned to the other side of the bed. She had to find a way to stop him from travelling.

Dodeye picked his mobile phone and made some business calls. Putting his house in order, Kokei thought.

He never made business calls before a trip to the village because he never stayed long enough.

"My love. Please don't leave yet. We can work this out, please. I beg you. For the sake of our children. Don't go."

Dodeye finished the call and made another.

She fell on her knees. "Doddies, you are not listening. Please."

"You never say sorry, do you?" He looked at her his voice as cold as steel. He closed his briefcase with a snap and lifted it easily. Picking the bag along with it, he headed for the door,

Kokei followed him. "Sorry for what? You refuse to tell me what I've done wrong. Please Dodeye, don't leave me for that girl. Please."

"Watch me. Say goodbye."

He slammed the door after him. Wisdom prompted her to follow him, drag him, beg, or do anything, everything possible to stop him. Instead, she lowered herself to the tiled floor, and watched her thoughts race ahead of him to Obandi.

CHAPTER-EIGHT

*D*ecember 1988, Calabar

Queen rotated her hips to the music blasting from her cassette player by Kool & the Gang, *Cherish*. Her gay mood contrasted the windy harmattan weather but definitely covered more of her uncertainty and fear but Queen was not one to be delayed when she was ready to do anything, particularly, to move on.

No one would believe they were fast approaching their third year away from home. She turned to stand in front of the mirror and examined herself. Her body had grown even more shapely and beautiful. At eighteen, she had matured tremendously and as a result of her desire to tone her skin, she looked even more mature. The toning had lightened her considerably even though she wasn't much prettier for all her efforts.

She opened her mouth and examined her teeth. They were in good order. For a moment, she smelt her breath and smiled. Now she was getting ready for the big scene. She swooned round and saw Giftie seated, staring at her.

She had been fast asleep when Queen walked in and put on the music.

"The music is too loud," Giftie murmured. "Okokon will come and be raving..."

"To hell with Okokon." Queen leaped. "I'm free like a bird, ha ha."

"What are you talking about?" Giftie slumped back on the bed. She had a splitting headache and the taste in her mouth fuelled her nausea. What the hell was wrong with her?

"I'm out of here, girl. And if you know what's good for you, you'd better get out too."

Queen was full of dreams about getting out, leaving the hotel, and working for herself. They were both tired of Okokon and his shady dealings, pimping them and cheating them. Yet, they'd never had enough to go away.

"To where?" Giftie said in a barely audible voice.

She hoped she wasn't pregnant. The pills Okokon gave her had worked wonders these past couple years and she had taken them religiously. She had promised herself she would not get pregnant again, unless she wanted the child, after the first and only abortion she did two years earlier.

The ordeal had almost taken her life.

Queen hissed. "What's wrong with you? Are you sick?"

"My period last month didn't come and this month is already overdue," Giftie said, close to tears. In almost three years of selling their bodies, Queen had not once gotten pregnant...or so she thought.

"There's a herbal treatment for delayed period," Queen said.

She went to her bag and brought out a small bottle of gin. The content was half-empty. She emptied it into a glass. She then took a lime from the small corner of the room they converted to a kitchenette, and squeezed one full lime into the gin. She mixed it before opening a sachet of white powdery substance, which she took from her handbag, the lime and gin mixture. She stirred the contents of the glass with a teaspoon for about 5 seconds.

She handed it over to Giftie. "Drink this."

"What is it?"

"You don't need to know. It's what I use when I miss my period. It never fails. By this evening, your visitor will visit as though running from a legion fountain." Queen laughed.

Giftie collected the mixture and stared at it she took a small sip and squeezed her faced.

"Drink it all up. Just close your eyes and down it," Queen said impatiently and checked her watch.

She went on her knees and pulled out a travelling bag from under the bed. She dropped it on the bed, and stood, arms akimbo, watching Giftie. Giftie drank the concoction as she had been told. She coughed once and clutched her stomach.

"Oh no!" She shouted and rushed to the bathroom. Queen laughed while Giftie heaved and emptied her bowels.

Giftie finally came out of the bathroom and leaned against the door. Queen had just about filled a big bag with her earthly belongings.

Giftie stared at her. "Where are you going?"

"To stay with Angela. Or Obal if you like."

"Obal? Your aunty? You found her?" Giftie staggered back to the bed. Strangely, she felt much better than she had felt in the past one month.

"Sure! I found her."

"Where? Okokon really tried to..."

"Don't mention that nit-wit's name around me. He had known her all along. He just didn't want to let us out."

"I'm coming with you." Giftie bent and looked under the bed before dragging out her own bag. The two girls packed in silence, each nursing her own deep thoughts.

Queen was thinking of what better opportunities lay ahead and how very lucky she was to be getting out of the hotel. She knew Okokon had bailed them out when they were stranded but then, they had more than paid for the help rendered. He had exploited them more than they could analyse and still, collected his weekly rent, twice reviewing it upwards.

Giftie was thinking of her dream to go to school. She had just saved enough to start a private afternoon school. With the contacts Okokon made for them, there was a regular income but what with this change, she may need to start all over again.

What if Obal or Angela would even exploit them more? Okokon had helped them and later fallen in love with her. But then, many of her clients claimed they loved her. Most of them were middle class, and she was really tired of her job. She couldn't wait to be through with school so she would get a job as a decent person. Five whorish years or more to go.

"Let's get out of here." Queen looked round briefly to check if there was anything left unpacked. Giftie followed suit.

"Okokon…"

"Please. If you want to stay…"

"I was about to say, he's going to suffer a heart failure," Giftie said, and the two girls burst into laughter.

They left the hotel room through a back door.

Angela's house was a two-bedroom flat she shared with two other girls. The house was going to be crowded though Angela was so sure the girls would soon be able to get their own place.

On seeing Angela, Giftie was shocked. Contrary to the impression that Angela was elderly, the girl was just a few years older than them. She would be twenty-one, at most, twenty-two.

Her hair was all curled up and cut short. The style made her look like an oversized baby but Giftie liked it. Angela herself was a pleasant person. She was like a breath of fresh air after being locked
up in a dungeon. Queen being the dungeon.

Angela's room was a world apart from what Queen and Giftie's room had been in the hotel.

It was spacious and well-decorated with soft pink and white wall paper. The floor was covered wall-to-wall with a thick ivory rug. A large bean bag with multi-colours sat in the middle of the floor.

Two cane chairs with two pink and white throw pillows each, rested against the wall at one end of the room, directly facing a simple wall cabinet, which also rested against the wall. A television set and a VCR were on the cabinet, with several framed pictures, and a flower vase containing plastic flowers.

Two large windows on corner adjacent were draped with beautiful baby pink curtains with lace lining. A three-in-one wardrobe, large enough to contain all their clothes and more sat next to a door leading to a toilet and bath. The bed was a sight to behold. Giftie marvelled at the king-size bed and mattress.

She had never seen anything so large and nice. She was sure the bed was at least three times the size of the one they'd had. And despite all the

furnishing in the room, there was still plenty of leg space.

After they unpacked amidst girl-chatter, Angela introduced them to the other girls in the house.

Regina and Glory were students in the university. Giftie warmed up to them at once. They had what she craved. After a meal together, the girls all retired to their different rooms.

"Obal, you must tell us how you got so rich! Your life is so beautiful. Your room is wonderful," Queen said eagerly.

Angela shrugged. "My dear, it wasn't easy! I started off in the hotel like you people, until I now had one client who fell in love with me. He was giving me lots of money and I stopped the hotel runs. We used to go out together, parties and all." She smiled. "He said he didn't want me working like that so he got one small room for me." She smirked. "But after sometime he tired me so I told him I was through. Like that like that, I had one boyfriend or the other till I met the one who owns this house. In fact, this one says he wants to marry me."

Queen's eyes widened. "Marry you! For real?"

Angela giggled. "For real. "Meanwhile, Obal is home-name o. Nobody knows me by that name here."

"Of course we understand. Who cares to bear home name around here. Hmm." Queen shook her head. "Thank God we found you. That idiot Okokon kept deceiving us."

Angela hissed "Okokon is a fool. He told me that you two came but refused to stay in the hotel. In fact, he said he took you back to the park and paid your fare back to Ugep. I should have known he was such a pathetic liar."

Giftie gasped. "You know Okokon?"

"Why your surprise, Giftie?" Queen hissed. "I had always told you he was no good." She turned to Angela. "Okokon made her believe he was in love with her, yet he gave her out to other men each night and even received commission!" Queen laughed and Angela joined in.

Giftie cringed. When would she ever learn all men were liars and deceivers?

CHAPTER-NINE

"Merry Christmas!"

Everyone chorused at once, and champagne began popping one after the other. The wind blew with a whistle sending the harmattan chill all around them as they congratulated themselves in the beautiful garden festooned with row upon row of Christmas lights. There must be hundreds of them.

Giftie looked round the garden in admiration and wonder. Strings of yellow, red and blue lights hung all around the trees in the garden, blinking with delight and precision.

At this time of the year, everything was usually dry and brown but this garden was green and well-watered. One could only imagine how much time and money must have been invested in caring for it.

Giftie thought of Angela, the chief hostess of this great Christmas party, and retired Colonel Effy Johnson, the chief host. The colonel was old enough to be Angela's grandfather. The retired-army-officer-turned-politician had his fill of the young raven he dated.

Angela was worse than a soiled dove by virtue

of what she had done in her life but to date such an old man was a departure from what Giftie had always known. And the old faggot was asking for marriage!

Giftie discovered the house they lived in had been deeded to Angela and the students were her tenants only because she didn't want to live all alone.

"Penny for your thoughts," a voice said behind her and she jumped, spilling some of her champagne.

"Sorry, I didn't mean to scare you," the owner of the voice, a young man, probably in his early thirties, said.

Giftie ran a quick appraisal of him. He would be about her height, thickset, dark complexion, simple, nice face, clean shaven. He wasn't attractive. Just an ordinary-looking well-dressed man.

She looked at his wristwatch, gold-plated. His shoes looked expensive and she noticed the confidence around his presence. She paid attention.

"Um, I'm alright. It's alright," she stammered.

She had been with Angela for two weeks now and despite the several parties they had attended,

she hadn't gotten hooked up yet. Queen, being who she was, was already dating two different men, a young civil servant and a middle-aged businessman. Angela had warned them to choose carefully. She planned to.

He came to stand in front of her. "So, how come a beautiful lady like you is here alone?"

Giftie picked her wits. "Well, perhaps I was waiting for a dashing young man like you."

He smiled. "Wooh, she is outspoken." He sipped from his glass and looked over the rim at her. "Is that an invitation?"

"Call it what would please you." She liked him. "What's your name?"

"Hah! Clever girl. Will you tell me yours if I tell you mine?" he said lightly.

"I'm Giftie," she said. "I don't play games." She turned round and moved toward the magnificent house, playing hard to get. In actual fact, she couldn't wait for him to follow her, chase her and win her. He looked like a choice man.

"I didn't mean to offend you," he said and followed her promptly.

She stopped and looked at him. "I'm not

offended."

He brought out his right hand for a shake. "I'm Emmanuel Ogar. I'd like to be your friend."

"Really, pleased to meet you." Giftie gave him her hand and he took it in a warm handshake.

He laughed. "Pleased to meet you too."

Emmanuel Ogar followed Giftie around the rest of the party and dropped her off in the early hours of the morning. He was a thirty-two-year old banker, an eligible bachelor, and Giftie felt she had hit her gold mine.

In the days that followed, she established a sweet relationship with him. Unfortunately, their love affair ended abruptly after Giftie told him her true story. She had thought she had found a soul mate. Emmanuel however, was not ready to marry a prostitute. Though she never confessed all she had ever done, he concluded from her stories about how she came to live in Calabar in a hotel for two years. She thought she could trust him, believed him when he told her he wanted to know her better. They had not even known each other for two weeks!

"Angela, leave her alone. She feels she knows all. She's just stubbornly foolish," Queen said after Giftie related her ordeal to her friends.

"You never understand, do you? You just feel every guy is bad. Emmanuel is a decent, caring and generous guy..."

Queen snapped. "That's why he threw your love in your face the day he discovered you were soiled."

"You two stop it." Angela said. "I think Giftie just needs experience to teach her the rules of engagement. Men who care too much about your past are better left alone." Angela counselled. "Otherwise, the insult will be too much."

"I guess I learnt one lesson there." Giftie sighed. Surprisingly, she discovered she hadn't had a tear to shed for Emmanuel Ogar. "It's just that he was so sweet for those few days we were together," Giftie said, full of regret.

"There are many fishes in the ocean," Queen said between clenched teeth.

"There are men like him all over town waiting to hook a very available girl like you," Angela said.

"Generous ones too. Ubong Edet is spoiling me foolish despite the fact that he knows he's not the only one."

Queen laughed. "Those *atam* men are generally too careful and jealous...."

Angela nodded. "And stupidly boring. Right now I don't have time for one. Couldn't be less careless."

Giftie sighed. "Emmanuel told me he wanted a wife. . ."

"And you think you are appropriate?"

"Leave her be, Queen. She'll learn," Angela said. "See, Giftie you'll learn."

Solomon Ansa came into Giftie's life a few days later. They had met at another party organised by Ubong Edet, Queen's heartthrob. He was eager to please and quite generous. Though single, he was not ready to settle down. It pleased Giftie well. This time, she made up a long story about her family being in the village, and spoke none of her eventful past.

Solomon showered her with a lot of attention and gifts and when Giftie enrolled in a private afternoon school for adults, he paid the bills. Despite several appeal to Queen to also follow suit, she refused. She and Angela dismissed education. It was, for them, a waste of precious time. Giftie refused to be disenchanted.

Life finally began to look up for Queen as well. Ubong, a self-employed and successful contract consultant, opened a gift shop for Queen and while she was busy messing around with several other men, he remained faithful to her, while being adequately unfaithful to his wife of six years.

Mid-June of 1989, Solomon's wife visited Giftie in her school. It was a dreary day, and the rain had been falling for three days consecutively, lightly but surely. The notorious Calabar rain was known to allow you leave your house, but its persistence would definitely soak you if you had no umbrella.

Mrs. Nkoyo Ansa was a rotund, woman with firm, fair-complexioned skin. She was much shorter than Giftie but where she lacked height, she gained for weight. She was bejewelled as though dressed for an important outing. Her face held a constant sulky pout.

Giftie was called out of her class to see the visitor. At first she thought it would be her mathematics teacher's wife. She had been having a secret fling with the forty-something-year-old man for some weeks and one or two other teachers were privy to the scandal.

Mrs. Ansa measured Giftie up with a steely gaze as the younger girl walked into the empty common room where she had been asked to wait.

Slender, tall maybe 5'8 or more, light-complexioned, beautiful, very beautiful. Graceful. Well-dressed. Well-composed. Almost classy. It was easy for anyone to understand at once what Solomon had seen in the pretty student.

Her next action did not connote much appreciation for the beauty displayed before her. She lunged for Giftie's middle region and with her weight, pushed the slim girl down. Yanking her neatly wrapped hair out of place, she knelt over her and dealt continuous blows to the girl's well made-up face.

Mrs. Ansa yelled profanities and angry curses as she raised her hand over and over. The sudden action took Giftie by shock and without knowing what to do apart from scream, she tried to block the heavy blows, while struggling to breathe under the weight of the heavy-muscled woman.

It took some time before anyone knew what was happening and by then, Giftie had almost fainted.

By the time they dragged the fat woman off her,

it seemed Mrs. Ansa had killed the girl. It could have been true but for the weak whimpering from Giftie.

The beating left her bedridden for one full week and out of school for another week. It was when she got back to school she learnt her assailant was her boyfriend's wife and not her "sugar daddy's" wife.

Solomon Ansa had lied to her about his marital status.

CHAPTER-TEN

January 2008, Calabar

The clouds gathered threateningly over the quiet suburbs of State Housing Estate. If it followed through to its expected end, it would be the first rain of the year. Kokei alone at home, after weeks of heat and harmattan dryness should be grateful for the change in weather, but she hadn't seen much to be thankful about in recent times.

Dodeye had come for the children shortly after the schools closed for the Christmas break, and left her alone in Calabar. He had put only one condition to her following them all to the village for the festivities - she would use the guest room since Obandi was with him in the master bedroom. Kokei had merely stared after him till he left with their three children.

What would she say?

It was the most dreadful holiday in her life. She dove into church activities to drown her sorrows.

He brought the children back to resume school only the previous week and they told her they stayed with their Grandma throughout the period

while "Daddy and his new wife" stayed in the country home.

Kokei was completely fluttered. Why would Dodeye do this to her? After all they had been through together over the years? Their wedding anniversary had passed unceremoniously. She had celebrated mournfully, alone, thinking of what her sweet husband was probably doing with the new wife.

Alone in their massive 8-bedroom sprawling mansion, she had had enough time to ruminate on her life. What had she done wrong? Where had she ever gone wrong? Since she gave her life to Christ, she had lived right. Not that there hadn't been temptations, there had been many, but God had helped her through them all.

What could one say of the faithfulness of God if after so many years of serving Him such a thing could happen?

She stood in front of her mirror and looked at herself.

For the first time, she noticed the lines around her eyes and mouth. She also noticed her collar bones jutted out and her flat stomach had flattened

more. She had lost considerable weight to say the least due to her extensive prayer and fasting.

Who wouldn't? She hadn't slept with her husband in three months! No, not that it mattered. What mattered was her husband was with someone else. She remembered he had teased her the previous year, before their troubles started that he wanted one more child. She had dismissed it. Now it bothered her. Had she taken in, would her husband still be with her? What more would one want after two sons and a daughter? Yet he had asked for one more child and she had refused.

The doorbell rang and she went to get the door. She had sent all the house staff away for the Christmas break and had told them all to take their time before coming back. Most travelled out of town after the famed Calabar Carnival. Not that it made a difference to Kokei.

It was Kommomo, her immediate younger sister. Kommomo was a widow.

At thirty-five, she looked young and marriageable but her marriage had been turbulent and she had opted to remain single with her eight-year-old daughter.

Kommomo worked as a junior staff in the University of Calabar Teaching Hospital and lived in the one-bedroom flat given by her sister's husband. The compound belonged to Dodeye Keyu, and as part of being the only free tenant, she acted as caretaker of the property. Hence paying her brother-in-law in kind rather than cash for the accommodation. When the problems had started between Dodeye and Kokei, she had remained as aloof as she could but when Dodeye left, she tried to intervene. It hadn't worked much.

"Momo," Kokei said wearily. "How are you?"

"Fine, Sister."

"*Awonke*. Come in." Kokei walked toward the living room, a spacious, homely room the family relaxed in.

The furniture was all soft and fluffy velvet, with throw pillows and bean bags strategically designed. The rug was thick enough to sink one's feet and fresh air came in from the open windows regally draped with designer curtains.

Everything about the living room spoke wealth and class.

Kokei closed the sliding windows and drew the curtains, throwing the room into semi-darkness, before switching on a chandelier and the air-conditioner. Kommomo sat easily in one of the seats.

"Sister, I have a feeling that someone is behind this problem you are having," Kommomo said.

"Let me get you a drink." Kokei moved toward the drink bar at one corner of the room but Kommomo shook her head.

"No, *sa-meh*. I am too burdened for a drink."

Kokei sighed. "Why do you feel like that?"

"My pastor was preaching on restitution last Sunday, and he spoke a lot about dealing with the past. It left me thinking that maybe it is someone you might have offended doing this to you..."

"I really don't understand you, Momo," Kokei stood and wiped her sweaty palms on her blue and yellow Vlisco skirt. She'd purchased the multi-coloured print material at Tinapa.

"I don't offend people. I haven't offended anyone since my rebirth. Who would want to hurt me?

"The past ten to twelve years have been used in service to God and humanity." Kokei shrugged.

"And anyway, why would anyone try and persuade my husband into taking a title. This is all spiritual. There mustn't be a reason for it."

Kommomo shook her head. "There may be. We should investigate this. Before you gave your life to Christ, did you offend someone?"

"Look Momo, I can't think of anyone. If you are so sure about this, maybe you should give me time to think about this. Where do I start from?" Kokei sat heavily.

"Maybe we should just pray about it!" Kommomo went to kneel before her sister and holding hands the two prayed together.

CHAPTER-ELEVEN

March 1991, Calabar

The girls tore at each other's faces as Angela crawled to one end of the room, screaming. She had never seen such madness in her life. The rain fell outside accompanied with loud thunders, and the electricity authority ceased power to cap it all up.

Regina and Glory banged on the door and threatened to break it down but their shouts went unnoticed.

Queen got a grip of Giftie's head and hit, once, twice against the wall. The third hit missed as Giftie used her knee on the other girl's stomach. The two rolled on to the floor, clawing, biting, punching, and then the door came down with a thud. Two watchmen in the compound crashed in with their lamps and pulled the two girls apart. Angela continued to sob hysterically. Queen and Giftie spat curses at one another, panting and struggling to be free in order to get at each other. It was 1.00a.m.

Giftie screamed. "She will kill all of us. This girl is mad. She is mad."

"Oh, you think you can get away because of your pretty face. I will claw out your eyes. Stupid girl," Queen said.

"This girl is bleeding!"

"Angela! Angela!" Glory screamed, rushing to the other girl. "Did they hit you?"

"Somebody get a motorcycle! Angela is bleeding."

"They are all bleeding. What a mess in this place. Was there an earthquake in here?"

"The whores were fighting themselves. Mad children. Broken bottles all over the place!"

"This girl needs medical attention. Blood all over her body..."

"Her cousin poisoned her. Queen is mad!"

"They were trying to abort. It wasn't a deliberate poisoning..."

All the girls were rushed to the hospital.

"Please contact Colonel for me," Angela said weakly before she passed out.

Effiong Bassey Okon entered the Amenity Ward of the University Teaching Hospital. Angela was in Room

3. The ward had only recently been built and still smelt of paint and new furniture, and of course,

hospital.

Angela was a sight to behold, with drips on her arm oxygen tubes over her face, and her legs hung up. Her head was wrapped with bandages and her eyes were shut tight.

"What happened?" Colonel said gruffly.

"We don't know exactly, sir. Only that the girls somehow got into a fight, she has cuts in her head inflicted by broken bottles. Her friends also have some broken bottle wounds... But that is not what makes her condition critical. She has been poisoned." The nurse on duty sighed. "Apparently she took some drugs that reacted with the alcohol she took. Her condition is very critical. She may not survive it."

Angela died a few days later. Cause of death was alcohol poisoning. Colonel Effiong Bassey Okon took up the case with the girls. They were arrested and detained for questioning, and later locked up. After over a week in police detention, Elder Ubi Ikpi came to bail the girls out. He was Queen's "sugar daddy's" good friend. In fact, he had made futile attempts to date Queen before but he had never met Giftie.

Elder Ikpi was a respectable citizen, and Managing Director of the newly established Equator Merchant Bank, the bank making waves in Calabar and Cross River State.

Elder Ikpi was also a chieftain in Ugep and an elder in his local church. In societal circles, he was well-known. He had been sent by his friend, Dr. Asuquo Ikpatt but despite his intervention, it wasn't much of good news for the two girls. Col. Okon had filed a murder charge against them. Their belongings were confiscated and they were not allowed to get access to their previous accommodation with the deceased Angela. They were stranded once again.

Elder Ikpi noticed the plight of the girls and took them to Dr. Ikpatt's residence.

"She can't stay here with me," Queen said sternly as they turned into the doctor's street.

Elder Ikpi looked incredulously at her "What?"

"Giftie cannot come with me. She's not welcome in Doctor's house," Queen said between her teeth.

"You're not staying here either," Elder Ikpi said, amused. "His wife is in town. I think he'll just arrange for somewhere to keep you two."

Queen stamped her feet. "I can't think of why he bailed her in the first place. She's the cause of all this mess! She killed Angela!"

"I bailed the two of you not Ikpatt. Now stop being so sulky," Elder Ikpi snapped.

As he had envisaged, Dr. Ikpatt could not accommodate the girls that night and after much deliberations, Elder Ikpi took them to his house. His wife, a nursing mother, was in bed when they arrived. Elder Ikpi introduced them as distant relatives from the village. His wife, unaware of any foul play entertained the young ladies.

But Queen and Giftie did not stay long in Elder Ikpi's hospitality. Early one morning about a week after they arrived from detention, Col. Okon's men came and arrested them. The girls were locked up in a military guard room, for another week. A hellish one. After the ordeal, Queen was advised to return to the village to escape the wrath of the colonel. Giftie decided to go back also but Elder Ikpi discouraged her.

"One of my tenants recently vacated a one-room apartment. I think I can give that to you," he offered generously.

"I can't pay, sir. I am really grateful but after what I've been through, I'd rather go back to Ugep," Giftie said, close to tears.

She had lost everything. Only her education was what she had to her credit and even that had earned her no qualification yet. She was back to nowhere. After five years of labouring, she had nothing!

He touched her cheek lightly. "I'm not asking for anything. I want to help you. You are a nice girl."

She shook her head. "Sir, Colonel Okon may come after me. I don't want to stay. I don't want to have to pay for the sins of Queen."

"Colonel Okon has been settled. He has dropped the charges. His only request was that Queen should disappear from Calabar."

"She didn't mean to harm Angela. Angela wanted to get rid of the pregnancy she had for one Inyang she didn't want Colonel to know about it. I warned Queen that Angela had taken some drugs to try and terminate the pregnancy but they didn't listen. She mixed the alcohol concoction for Angela and after she took it started throwing up blood…"

Giftie started to sob.

"It's alright. We know the story, that's why the colonel is dropping all the charges. It has been concluded as accidental death since Queen did not know about the drugs..."

"I can't stay, sir, I'd rather go back home."

"I will take care of you. Don't worry." He pulled her into his arms and hugged her tight. "Will you allow me to take care of you?"

Giftie knew what he was asking and she shuddered at the thought. What better life did she hope to have? Back in the village, things were pretty much the same for her mother and sisters. And her mother had even asked that she take Kommomo her immediate younger sister, with her. She was three years older than Kommomo and her mother could not force any request on her. She had only sent money home twice but that was enough to create an impression about her - she was doing well.

How she made it was of no consequence, and with a one-room apartment, Kommomo could join her in Calabar. She could also continue her education.

Just two and a half more years to go and she would bag her WAEC and enter the university. She would be on her way to earning a degree and living respectably. Just a few more years and she would be free from the bondage of men. She promised herself she would never marry. Maybe have one or two kids from different men. That way, she wouldn't be tied to any of them.

"Elder, you are my only salvation." She rested her head snugly on his chest. He was a heavily built man with a small potbelly. His angular face was well-shaven always with only a thin moustache. He was in his early forties, actively in the prime of his life. Giftie hoped this decision would take her to the end of her studies.

"I need to ask you something, now that you are my ur...responsibility," he said softly.

"I am at your service," she said.

"I don't like your name. I will call you Joy...because you are my joy."

She pressed closer. "I will always be your joy."

From Kokei, to Giftie, now Joy; each name with a different story. What more surprises did life hold for her?

CHAPTER-TWELVE

The day was an unusual one. The new yam festival was not yet due and preparations were underway. Still, the town of Ugep usually lively, was serene. Sober, the clouds had gathered and daylight resembled night. This particular heaven will empty with a vengeance when it finally did, Queen thought miserably. She lay cuddled on her mat in her corner of the room.

The Ekpodem cults had visited the chiefs to make important alliances. They would discuss war. War. Her father had died in the last land boundary war with Adim. They had lost very few men and her father had been one of them. Why? She felt miserable. As useless and wicked as he had been, she still missed him. Her mother had told her an *Ekpodem* would marry her. She cringed at the idea. They were a new cult from Biase local government area, who came to meet with the village head to discuss and enter into an arrangement for war protection.

They were dangerous people. Queen could not imagine what life with one could be.

History believed members to be immortal. An initiated member could not be penetrated by a bullet or a knife. A typical member bore a mark of the cult, which was a cut in their flesh with a treated razor blade.

She heard loud drumbeats outside the house, and as she curled closer to herself, the drum beat louder. The sound grew closer and closer and with it she heard bells clanging, feet shuffling. She suspected some masquerade must be passing by but had no desire to go outside to watch. Or do anything for that matter.

She remembered her years in Calabar with shame. She remembered Kokei with bitterness. Her life then had been better. She was tired of village life. The sound of the troop passed and she listened for the drumbeat as from a distance. Lightning and thunders began to strike and suddenly the rains came, just as Queen had expected, with a vengeance. She felt all the loneliness she had bottled up burst and before she knew it, she was weeping.

She sat up and hugged her knees to herself. The room was still as it had always been.

Two mats folded up at one corner of the room belonged to her brother Ushi and sister, Evechi. Avakpa, her other sister had gotten married while she was away. Two other brothers had long since left home. No one knew where they were. No one cared. A simple cupboard with six compartments housed their meagre supply of clothes. On it lay a simple store of toiletries. Two old worn out travelling bags were stuffed behind the folded mats.

A stupid thought flashed across Queen's mind but fled as soon, to return to Calabar. She had no money. And nobody. Calabar was a no-go for her and Uyo seemed so far to travel alone...and she thought of Kokei again. What was she doing now? Probably in school! School! She wished she had gone to school if only for two or three years. She would have been able to teach in the new mission's primary school. Then no one would think of marrying her off to an *Ekpodem*.

She hated Kokei for betraying her. Under pressure she had told the truth. Implicating her. What could have become of her if Elder Ikpi had not intervened?

She let out a churlish sound as she cursed Kokei.

A door banged open and she jumped. Her mother came in with Ushi, carrying some wet firewood. They were both soaked through.

"What are you doing here?" her mother said, shocked at seeing her alone.

"Mama, welcome," Queen said sullenly.

Onache, her mother, gave her one bland look and hissed before moving into the adjoining room she had shared with her husband for over twenty years.

"Where's Evechi?" Onache called out.

The rustling sound indicated she was probably changing into dry clothes. Her voice etched with impatience. She was always impatient with all of them.

"I don't know," Queen muttered but loud enough.

"What is eating at you? Is it this issue of marrying Ekpeyong that you are so angry about?" Onache came out tying a wrapper round her chest. "You are a foolish girl. After wasting all your life in Calabar, you are not even grateful that someone will want to marry you!" Onache hissed again.

"Where is that little slut that took you away from your family? Kokei or what is her name?

"That girl was the end of you, like mother like daughter. If not for the intervention of our fathers..."

Queen snapped. "Mama, cut off the details. I just need to be left alone."

"Not for long my dear." She took a piece of kola in her hand and bit into it, pausing to savour it. "Ekpeyong is coming back this night to pay your bride price, after they dance back from the shrine, and finish the rituals."

Queen raised her head. "I cannot marry an *Ekpodem*, Mama. I will run away!"

"You will go nowhere," Onache said easily. "He has a spell on you. In fact, you will remain cuddled up in this room till he comes for you." Onache laughed.

"I will go nowhere with Ekpeyong!" Queen screamed. She cuddled up even more on the mat, and folded her hands over her head.

"Look at you! Kokei is enjoying her life, making progress, doing well. Her harlot mother is wearing expensive clothes and thanking her stars, flouting

her beautiful hind all over the village.

"Don't you think? Is it a man's cult that will stop you from being his wife...?"

"He is not educated!"

"Are you? You'd better pull yourself together. Come look at the expensive wrapper he bought for this occasion! You are luckier than you ever deserve. You should think of your friend Kokei and thank your stars."

"Curse Kokei! Don't ever mention her in my presence."

CHAPTER-THIRTEEN

July 2008, Calabar

The rain poured as heavily as the clouds had warned. Kokei, dressed in a simple Hollandaise wax blouse and long skirt, threw a shawl round her neck for a little warmth. From her balcony upstairs, she called on the driver, Akpan, to bring the vehicle to the front.

Kommomo, who had stayed back at her sister's house for over six months, was already dressed in a navy blue and black flowing dress and waiting downstairs in the lobby. Kokei knew she was taking a bold step, but it was one needed to be taken.

The sisters picked Atai in her house on their way out. Despite the bad weather, the grey Lincoln Navigator took intricate wetness of the road with ease and balance.

Kokei fidgeted throughout the trip while Kommomo tried to calm her down. With the chilling air-conditioner in the jeep, she found herself sweating profusely.

At one point, she was tempted to stop Akpan and go into the rain.

She needed cleansing. And something, anything to take the jumpy feeling away.

Her mind roamed over the events of the past few months. Taking to Kommomo's advice, she had drawn up a list of the people she might have offended. It had cost her no small stress. The list seemed endless. Together, the two sisters had prayed over the list and eliminated some names. Names of people who Kokei had apologised to earlier were eliminated. Other names of people who most likely wouldn't know she had offended them were also removed. Elder Ikpi was long dead, so he was removed from the list. Kokei was left with three names.

Mrs. Solomon Ansa. Who had confronted her several times over one year of her relationship with her husband. Who had rained curses on her several times, cursed her womb and married life. Who had sworn Kokei will never have peace in life as long as she lived. Who had finally been forced out of her matrimonial home on Kokei's account.

Mrs. Ansa was found living with her grown son in the outskirts of Calabar town, squatting in her widowed aunt's 2-bedroom bungalow at the Atimbo

Navy Barracks.

When Kokei got there with Kommomo and Pastor Bassey's wife, Atai, Mrs. Ansa, her aunt and son were all present at home, and they welcomed them howbeit with caution. Mrs. Ansa did not recognise any of the women but after Atai introduced the party, Mrs. Ansa went into a rage, cursing and lunging at Kokei.

Kokei jumped up, ready to take off, but Atai stopped her before she got to the door.

"We came here to apologise, and for restitution," Atai said, as advocate between a trembling Kokei and the offended hostess. Kommomo remained in her seat.

Mrs. Ansa cursed. "Restitution of what?"

"Wait," the elderly aunt held up her hand and Mrs. Ansa fell silent. "Tell us what you propose."

"We hope to apologise and ask her to revoke any curses she placed on Kokei. You see, Kokei has repented and is truly sorry."

Mrs. Ansa screeched. "Is that all? Apologise? My marriage broke up and all you can do is apologise!"

Her aunt moaned. "She will forgive you but you must bring something, a gift to appease her."

"I am ready to give her anything. I am truly sorry—"

Mrs. Ansa's son bellowed, interrupting Kokei. "What do you have to give?" He couldn't be more than twenty-five years though he looked and sounded much older.

"I can make out a cheque for half a million—"

Mrs. Ansa's aunt's eyes bulged. "Half a million?"

"Half a million for twenty years of misery caused by you? Please leave this place and don't insult us." The son bit out. His mother tapped him. His grand-aunt rolled her eyes.

"How much do you want?" Kommomo surprised them further by asking.

The boy blinked. "Two million."

Mrs. Ansa's mouth drooped.

Kokei brought out a cheque book and pen from her bag and scribbled the amount. "For Mrs. Ansa?"

The words came out in a stutter. "Mrs. Margaret Ansa."

"You have to revoke the curse on her and bless her," Atai said.

"Come and kneel in front of me." Mrs. Ansa's voice trembled. Kokei gave her the cheque and she took it with shaky fingers.

Blessing such as Margaret Ansa had never prayed for herself poured forth from her lips over Kokei's kneeling frame.

The following month, Dodeye came home to Calabar with Obandi. The trio: Dodeye, Obandi and Kokei slept in different rooms.

***

Kokei picked the second person on her list, Okokon, determined Margaret Ansa's prayers were not working. She knew she might have offended him because she had gone with part of his money when she left the hotel. Okokon might have placed a curse.

It took her over two months to locate Okokon's family. And even then, they told her Okokon had died over seven years previously. Whatever curse he might have placed on her was dead and gone. She explained her situation to his wife and gave her a cheque for fifty thousand naira.

She moved to the last name on her list. Isalo. She had not heard from Isalo ever since they parted ways. Her mother had told her Isalo got married and moved to Biase but Wofai, her little sister, discovered Isalo was back in Ugep, taking care of her sick mother.

Kokei, Kommomo and Atai went to visit Isalo. As they negotiated the final bend before the entrance of the village, Kokei took Atai's hand and they both spoke words of prayers. Softly from the front seat, Kommomo sang hymns.

The sun was high up by the time they entered Isalo's family compound. Kokei remembered the compound with trepidation. Nothing had changed. The mud building plastered with cement had only deteriorated with more of the cement plastering off. Otherwise, everything looked just the same. She had lived in this house, she thought wearily.

Isalo sat on the frontage, sieving corn for pap. She tied a worn-out wrapper about her chest, while straps of a black bra showed off on her shoulders. Her hair, permed but with thick undergrowth black, shining and long was tied into two knots with a centre-part, looked unkempt.

She looked up when the Lincoln parked by the roadside in front of the compound. Isalo had not changed in the eighteen years Kokei saw her last, except for a few stress lines on her face.

They approached the house, and Isalo stopped what she was doing completely and stared.

The frown on her face suggested she couldn't recognise the people approaching her. Atai led the way, followed by Kommomo. Kokei walked up slowly behind them.

"Effaemiode!" She called and a young lady, about seventeen years old came out quickly as though she had been hunching behind the door, waiting for her summons. "Bring seats for our guests," she said.

Atai spoke. "Good morning."

"Eh—eh. I don't know you people—"

Effaemiode came back with three small stools held clumsily in her hands. She glanced at the guests with her thick lips drooping. She was a splitting image of Isalo, though much younger and prettier. Kokei concluded she would be Isalo's daughter.

"We are not strangers either," Atai said.

Isalo looked at them one by one and came to rest on Kokei. Light of recognition lit her eyes and then dimmed into slits.

"You may not sit down," she said between her

teeth. "Kokei Leko!" She snapped, deliberately using the latter's maiden name. "What do you want with me?"

"Forgiveness." Kokei fell to her knees on the dust floor, lumps of tears choked her speech. "I need your forgiveness. Please."

Isalo startled, and the sting in her bitter voice tempered. "For what?"

"No one knows what happened that night Angela died but I know I have offended you by implicating you..."

"Abeg! If that is what is chasing you about you'd better go and sleep. I don't have time for petty talk..." She looked Kokei over. "With rich women. You want nothing to do with me and the feeling is mutual."

"Please let bygone be bygone," Atai said.

"Bygone is bygone. Please leave this place. Why would you even seek my forgiveness? Your life is good, isn't it? Your husband has been doling out millions," her voice hardened. "Please get out of here."

"I don't have peace, Isalo," Kokei said close to tears. "My husband left me. There's money but no

joy. I prefer to have my peace and joy than all this wealth..."

"Shut up. Why won't you say that? Do you know the first thing about poverty? If your husband has left, why don't you go after him? What has this got to do with me?" Isalo resumed her chore.

"Do you know anything about his activities since he took the new wife?" Kokei said.

Her knees ached but she had no desire to stand up yet. She knew Isalo had not changed. She could probably know something.

The sieve in Isalo's hand dropped in heated anger and she looked at Kokei with hatred so thick one could almost taste it in the air.

"Do I know...? Are you mad?" Isalo snapped, giving no regard to Kokei or the ladies with her. Not caring about who they were or that her old friend and worst enemy remained on her knees.

"Please, this is no longer a child's play. I am Kommomo, Kokei's sister and she has been through hell. You were her first friend and though things went wrong between you two, you may find the root of this problem. Please." Kommomo went on her knees beside Kokei. "If you placed a curse on

her, we beg you, revoke it. This torture is too much."

Isalo clapped and hissed. "Shut up your mouth! So you are that Kommomo. Go! All of you have eaten Keyu's money now it is beginning to purge you. I did not place any curse. It is the works of Kokei's hands that is following her. Nemesis always catches up." She laughed but stopped abruptly, her face twisted into a wicked smirk. "Go to Obol Otoma's compound. His daughter may have stories to tell you. Now, get out of here and don't ever come back or I will place that curse I should have placed long ago."

Kokei snapped. "Obol Otoma..."

Isalo yelled. "Get out of my house."

Atai and Kommomo jumped up and Kokei followed more slowly.

"Thank you, and God bless you. We will come back to say thank you again," Atai said.

"Don't ever come back here," Isalo mumbled, refusing to look up until she heard their receding footsteps.

When she finally did look up, there were tears in her eyes. And a deep hatred in her heart.

CHAPTER-FOURTEEN

July 1993, Calabar

Throngs of people moved in and out of the faculty office, some joyfully, some tearfully. Joy pulled Elder Ikpi along excitedly. She couldn't wait to be back in her house for the celebration that followed though out in the sun and in the open air, she jumped on the Elder's neck and laughed. Elder Ikpi caught her by her waist and swung her round. A few passers hissed at the open affront but the couple ignored them.

"Now you have your papers complete, I think I will have to do something drastic to keep you in my arms knowing how hot *Unical* babes are in the market."

"Darling..."

"Ssh." He put a finger to her lips. "I've lived in this town longer than you. I will spoil you." He placed a quick kiss on her lips and shoved her forward gently.

"I can never love another man…" she whispered soberly, her beautiful eyes sweltering.

"Don't try and discourage me. I am going to survive in a competitive market," he said.

"Com'on. I have a surprise waiting for you in your house." His hand rested lightly on her hip bone as they strolled toward his 1983 model Datsun Bluebird.

"Really?" She shrieked. "You knew I was going to pass?"

"You're too beautiful to fail," he said.

She skipped. "I will say a special thank you. What is the surprise?"

"Then it wouldn't be a surprise anymore. And the thank you will also not be so special. Now that is what I can't wait for," he said, his gaze travelling down her face and body.

She threw her head back, and laughed. "Chief chief."

They got to his car, and he opened the door for her.

He drove a little too fast but she loved it.

A new Volkswagen was parked in front of her one-bedroom flat. The car was sky blue, her favourite colour. Before the Datsun had stopped fully, she jumped out of it.

"Yes, little girl. This is your surprise."

For the second time in just a few minutes, Joy jumped on the elder's neck but this time, he caught her on. His mouth descended on hers in a passionate kiss, and they clung to each other.

His head came up just long enough to say, "Now for my special thank you."

"Honey, I can't even drive," she said shakily, conscious her neighbours could be watching.

Not that they were doing anything new. She was the landlord's woman in the beautiful compound with four one-bedroom apartments. Who cared? On more than one occasion, Elder Ikpi had exposed her body on her balcony while in the heat of passion. To all who lived in the compound, the two male bankers who shared the flat opposite hers; the family of four who lived adjacent to them; and the widowed mid-wife and her three adolescent sons who lived adjacent to her, she was the landlord's whore, and a force to reckon with. No one messed with her. No one mixed with her. Even her sister, Kommomo, who now lived with her, knew her limits.

"Thank me for this one, and I'll teach you to drive the car," Elder Ikpi said.

***

Joy learnt to drive within a week and did all her shopping for the university with her car. She had been given admission to study Marketing at the University of Calabar. She decided to guard her relationship with Elder Ikpi jealously. More than anything, he had made her, she vowed her life to serving him.

She realised he was her security and she would rather be nowhere else. On one of his numerous visits to her house, after serving him a sumptuous dinner, and they relaxed on the couch in her parlour, she decided to let him know her thoughts and desires.

"Marry me," she told him. "I will be your third wife, I don't care. I love you."

"I know, baby. I love you too but marriage, is something..."

She stepped back. "Something? What?"

"You don't love me enough. We are only using each other, don't forget that. I am not a child, Joy. I know what I enjoy from you and what you enjoy from me...we both shouldn't complain. I am content and I am a lucky man to have you. All my friends

are envious."

She shook her head. "I want to be your wife, Chief. I love you so much, I'd die before I lose you," she cried.

"Then you would never die, because won't lose me."

"Chief, no. I want marriage." She shrugged. "I don't mind remaining here, even as your wife."

"No."

"Chief, give me a child then let me have something from you."

He pressed his finger on her lips and increased the volume of the television to listen to the evening news. "Stop talking," he said.

For the first time since she got to Calabar, Joy truly felt defeated. She resolved then that even if he wouldn't marry her, she would get pregnant for him and have children for him. To carry out her plans, she stopped taking her contraceptive pills, without informing Elder Ikpi and she never talked about the proposal again.

Shortly before the end of the academic session Joy discovered she was pregnant. She was elated. She decided to keep the good news to herself at the

initial stage but her joy was short-lived.

She got a message from Ugep her mother was sick. Mma had been diagnosed with symptoms of a strange disease called AIDS. Joy was shattered. She had never heard of the disease and when she saw the doctors, the news was indeed bad. There was no cure for AIDS. Mma would die, a most humiliating and painful death.

Elder Ikpi and Joy travelled to visit Mma and found her in a pitiable condition. They immediately took her back to Calabar. She spent one full month in the hospital before her death. At the news of her passing, Joy fainted but was revived, bleeding. She lost her pregnancy in the process, and Elder Ikpi had never even known.

CHAPTER-FIFTEEN

Mma's burial was a showcase. Ugep town shook to its roots. Elder Ikpi buried her as though she were his own mother. Dignitaries from all over the country attended and Joy played hostess to the high and mighty in society. It was an occasion the community would not forget soon.

The service of songs started on Thursday night. The church, in whom Mma had been a devout member, buried her. The night was cool and it drizzled continually throughout the service. There was vigil night on Friday, where the four daughters of the deceased with their friends and family sang and danced through the night. Mma had later had a son after Wofai, her last daughter, but the father of the boy had taken him away from her when the boy was barely two years old. Neither father nor son showed up at the ceremony.

Saturday morning, Mma was laid-in-state. Dressed in a white wedding dress, she looked as though she merely slept. She was truly beautiful even in death.

The four daughters and Elder Ikpi and Womi's mechanic husband Akedo, wore white lace and sat in the room with her corpse while mourners thronged in to pay their last respect, and to sympathise with the family. None of the girls' fathers showed up.

At the graveside, Joy wept like a baby, screaming her mother's name over and over.

An interment followed in Elder Ikpi's country house and a night party was organised in the evening. The party also lasted all through the night, and a thanksgiving service was held on Sunday morning at the church. Later in the evening, after the guests had all gone, the girls gathered for a meeting. Elder Ikpi and Akedo were also present.

"We have to distribute mother's things," Joy said. "And I'll suggest that Womi and Wofai look into that so we know what is on ground."

"Are we keeping the house?" Wofai asked.

"We don't have accommodation right now and we hope to keep the place," Womi said, glancing nervously at her husband.

"If you will pay for it," Akedo said sternly, his gaze locked on hers.

"What is the condition of the house? Is the rent due? Give me details." Elder Ikpi referred his question to Joy, who looked at Wofai.

"Well, Mama used to pay monthly and since she fell ill, we've been owing for over five months. The landlord is very angry. I can't foot the bill since I just started the apprenticeship tailoring. So...well, Womi and..."

"You know we are not in the position." Womi cut in harshly. "We stay in the workshop where Akedo work s..."

"If you can just pay for the room. It's only fifty naira a month. Chicken change for people like you!" Akedo spat out. There was a tensed silence for a moment.

Elder Ikpi broke the silence. "Wofai, I'll ask you to make enquiries about purchase of the house."

Joy exclaimed. "Purchase? Chief!"

Akedo snickered. "You think you can buy the place? The landlord will never sell. Pay a year's rent and we can cope after that."

"Akedo, are you not even grateful..." Joy started angrily.

"Sister, please leave him. Ignore him. He's always like that," Wofai whispered.

"Well, find out as Chief has asked..."

"If possible, today. So that we can make the arrangements before we leave tomorrow," Elder Ikpi said matter-of-fact.

"Thank you so much, Chief," Joy said.

Womi and Wofai thanked the Elder simultaneously while Akedo merely sneered.

"I think you should know, Chief, that the 'house' is just a room in a compound of about three or four bungalows. The landlord stays in one of the other bungalows," Joy said.

"Let's just find out how much the landlord will sell the whole lot," Elder Ikpi said.

The following month, Elder Ikpi paid a ridiculous three hundred thousand naira for the compound in Joy's name.

Joy celebrated her twenty-fifth birthday in style that year. Elder Ikpi had wanted her to mark it at Christmas but she wanted an exclusive party on her day. He had to travel out of the state and so he made the necessary arrangement for a poolside party at the Metropolitan Hotel.

On the 'D' day, Joy wore a lovely lilac chiffon mini-dress and high stilt slippers.

Her face was lightly made up to highlight without unduly pronouncing her soft, beautiful eyes, and sensuous full lips. Her long permed hair was set and styled in cascading waves, left free for the late afternoon breeze to toy with, the style further exposing her beautiful face. There were several guests in attendance, many of whom were her friends, and Joy looked like a beauty queen. The weather was crisp and windy, the early harmattan season setting in.

Guests were served with food and drinks and pop music played in the background consistently. The M .C. announced the birthday girl was about to take the dance floor and called for the young men to take a ballot on who would take the first dance with her. The lot fell on a dashing, young man Joy had never met before. He would be in his mid-thirties, maybe younger. He really looked ageless. He was tall, dark, with smooth, strong features. His lips especially caught Joy's attention. They were beautiful on a man, as he smiled at her and took her in his arms for a swing to Madonna's "Laisla Bonita."

Joy liked the smell of him, and the feel of him,

and she pressed herself close. After the first dance, she danced with some of her classmates and other friends and then walked up to the first guy to take another dance. While Lionel Richie sang "Penny Lover," Joy imagined what it would be like to be this guy's lover.

She moved back a little as the dance came to a close. "I don't even know your name."

"Dodeye Keyu."

"Nice name. Can you swim?" she asked as they left the dance floor.

The party progressed considerably. Many of the guests changed into their swimsuits and went into the pool. Some lounged lazily, munching and sipping. The sun set and the garden lights were turned on giving the poolside a romantic hue.

Dodeye Keyu smiled. "Yes, and you?"

"A little." She winked. "Why don't you change, and maybe show me one or two things I don't know about swimming."

"My pleasure."

After that night, Dodeye Keyu visited Joy in her flat. She categorically told him not to repeat the gesture.

"My uncle will be mad. He is so protective of me. He's out of town now but he'll be back next week. I don't want his trouble," she said.

"Doesn't he know you're of age?" he teased.

"Since my mother died a few months back, he's been over-protective."

"I'm sorry about your mother."

Joy shrugged. "It's alright."

"So how do I see you? I mean, this lurking uncle is going to hinder me. And I really want to know you better."

Joy sighed. "I don't know..."

"I'm new in town and I'm staying at this newly established Marian Hotels and Towers. Will I be asking for too much if I suggest that you check me there?" he asked.

Joy's heart did a somersault. She liked this man already. She would do anything to please him.

"Well." She shrugged modestly. "I guess that wouldn't reduce my marketability too much."

"You're such a sweet girl. Tell me," he smiled at her, "do you have a native name?"

"Yes, but I...well. It's Kokei."

"Kokei! Gift. That is a very sweet name. It fits you much better than Joy. Why don't you bear it? Don't tell me you didn't know the meaning of it!"

"Not at all." Joy smiled. "It's just that we all have this mentality it's the village name and well..."

"That's nonsense. Kokei fits you much better than any other name. Can I call you Kokei?"

"Definitely. Anything you want."

CHAPTER-SIXTEEN

July 2008, Calabar

Kokei, Kommomo and Atai spent the night in Kokei's country home. It was a restless night. The trio spent most of the time singing and praying, seeking the face of God concerning their visit to the Obol Otoma's compound.

The following day, they got ready early and visited the Obol Otoma. Obol Otoma was a title chief, and one of the three high chiefs next to the Obol Lopol. Dodeye's father was also one of the high chiefs and it was his chieftaincy the council now offered to Dodeye.

Under the custom, there was nothing like resignation in the Obol Lopol's council but with development and enlightenment, a lot of the native customs were being changed and overlooked. Otherwise, Dodeye would probably not even be eligible to sit in the Obol Lopol's council.

Obol Otoma Ofem was a powerful chief in Ugep, who also sat in council with some lesser chiefs. As the Lincoln swerved smoothly into his large compound, Kokei developed cold feet.

She didn't even know what to expect.

Contrary to the previous night's rains, the sky was clear, and the day promised to be sunny and bright. It contrasted with Kokei's morale.

Obol Otoma Ofem, a man in his late 70s sat in council when they arrived. After what seemed like forever, they were summoned into his private chambers by a middle-aged woman, who Kokei recognised at once as the elder who sat with Obandi on the day of her presentation to Dodeye.

Kokei really couldn't understand why the Obol Otoma would be in anyway involved in her predicament. Atai made herself the spoke-person again. After elaborate greetings, she got down to the business of the day. They were served with kolanuts, garden egg with groundnut paste, and assorted drinks.

"Sir, my name is Atai Bassey. I am a pastor's wife. I have come with Kokei Keyu and her sister Kommomo because we have been directed to seek your help about the marital problems Kokei is having..."

The woman stood. "Papa, please excuse me."

"Nneoyi, sit down," Obol Otoma said without looking at her. Kokei felt the tension build at once.

"Who directed you to come here?" the Obol Otoma asked, looking from Kokei to Atai.

"An old friend of mine. Her name is Isalo," Kokei answered.

"Ha! Isalo, the self-made town-crier." Obol Otoma laughed. "So, what help do you seek?"

"My husband just took a chieftaincy title in the village and a second wife, which you are aware of, sir. I am so confused. I need help to get him back. I need to know if I am operating under a curse or not. Dodeye was a devoted husband and father but suddenly this came up..." Kokei sniffed.

The woman burst into laughter and hissed. For a moment, Kokei stared at her, expecting a comment but when the woman pressed her lips together and stared ahead, she continued her lamentation.

"I am under torture. I have no peace," she said. "I know you can talk to Dodeye. I know you are a close friend of his father." Kokei went on her knees.

"And also he is Obandi's grandfather." The woman smirked. "Woman, you have come to the wrong place. Go and retrace your steps to your days as a whore, painting the city of Calabar red with your whoredom, and wickedness. Give me a break. See who is talking about torture.

"Suddenly, the oppressor is being oppressed." She laughed. "Papa, I told you she'll come. Please excuse me." She stood.

"Nneoyi, sit down," Obol Otoma said a second time and Nneoyi obeyed howbeit grudgingly. "Since she has finally come as you said she will, then you have to forgive her."

"Forgive, Papa. Is that not taking it too far? Where do I start with forgiving her?"

"You can start by telling her what she did to you." Obol Otoma looked at Nneoyi. "You can start by demanding an apology, a restitution."

"Papa, restitution is what she has now. Will my husband whom she used and finished come back? Can my peace and matrimony which she took and discarded ever return? Can my Obandi, the sacrifice, already with child, come back as a virgin? There's nothing to forgive. No room for restitution!"

"Please, who are you? Tell us, please. We are sorry. Please. If there is a curse on Kokei, please revoke it. We beg you." Kommomo went on her knees, close to tears. Atai joined the other two in the kneeling supplication. Kokei gasped, too confused to speak.

"Our elders say that a child does not know evil concoctions. Instead he calls it vegetable soup, Papa. Please let me go in and finish my chores. If I could bear the brunt of Kokei's fires, then she should persevere and bear the brunt of my ministrations. Sacrificing my only daughter, Obandi. She still wins, Papa. She wins."

Nneoyi bursts into tears and this time when she stood and excused herself for a third time, her father did not stop her. She ran in, her deep sobs echoing through the house.

Tears coursed down Kokei's cheeks. To imagine she didn't even still know who she had offended! She gripped her chest and struggled to hold a sob.

"Kokei, that woman is my daughter. Her late husband is someone you know very well. His name?" Obol Otoma Ofem stood and staggered a little before regaining his balance. He looked at the three kneeling ladies with sad eyes. "His name? Elder George Ikpi."

He turned and slowly walked into his house, leaving the three gasping, Kokei choking and,

clutching her mid-region.

CHAPTER-SEVENTEEN

December 1994, Calabar

Elder Ikpi came back from his conference in Lagos just in time for Christmas. He had promised Joy he would make it up to her for his absence at her twenty-fifth birthday. Hence, he booked three nights at the Obudu Cattle Ranch to span the Christmas period.

On the 24th, he travelled with Joy all the way to the Ranch. Joy was sullen and preoccupied throughout the treat. What puzzled the Elder the most, was her refusal to have sex with him.

In fact, he virtually raped her on Christmas day. By the time they returned to Calabar on the 27th, Elder Ikpi's mood was as dark as hers. He wondered what could have been the problem. He wondered if Joy was seeing someone else, but dismissed the thought as soon as it came.

He didn't have long to wait to find out.

The first thing Joy did on New Year's Day of 1995 was to drive the Volkswagen he gave her right into his compound. She drove so roughly she hit the car against part of the wall of the gate, smashing

blocks and condemning of the car.

The crash brought the family out; Elder Ikpi at home with his wife, two adolescent sons and a toddler daughter.

Joy got out of the car with a slam. Elder Ikpi's countenance fell, his face contorted with shock. She strolled to the front of the house, swaying her hips outrageously.

"Hello, everybody!" She greeted cheerily and stood in front of Elder Ikpi, dangling the key of the car in his face.

It was mid-morning and the sun glowed in its full glory. Beads of sweat gathered on the Elder's forehead and nose, and trickled down. What was happening?

"Surprise everyone. Chief, happy new year."

"Joy, come in," Elder Ikpi said.

His wife glared at him, surely expecting an explanation. His fifteen-year-old son came to stand beside him while the eleven-year-old and the three-year-old girl, stood with their mother, close to the entrance behind him.

"No, I can't come in. I'm in a hurry. I came to tell you, I don't need your car anymore. I don't

need your money anymore.

"I am calling it quits between us. I'm getting married, Chief." She rolled her eyes. "Finally."

"Daddy, who is this?" His first son asked.

For the first time Elder Ikpi looked at his family, one by one, and then turned to look at Joy. She was already leaving. The key of the Volks on the ground in front of him.

"Joy!" He called and followed her.

"Don't call me that name. My fiancé hates it!" She shouted without stopping or looking back.

Elder Ikpi half-ran after her. "Joy, get into this car and let's go somewhere to talk."

"Sorry, too late." She waved him off and as she got to the gate, turned back. "Sorry, about your gate," she said.

A Grey Volvo 244 Gl waited for her outside the gate. Elder Ikpi stopped short from pursuing her as she entered the car and gave the driver a quick kiss before the car zoomed off.

***

Mrs. Ikpi went back into the house, with her children. Her heart heaved as she made a conscious effort not to burst into tears. What had she not

done to keep her home?

She had suspected her husband was cheating, she had just never suspected it would be with such a young lady. He would be more than twenty years older than the girl. A car! He had bought a car for her when his wife and kids moved around town mounting taxis and buses. She felt physical pain in her heart.

Elder Ikpi followed his family into the house but instead of offering an explanation, he went into his room, changed into fresh clothes and taking the Volkswagen, zoomed out of the compound without even stopping to inspect the damages done to the walls of his gate. His wife knew he had gone after the girl and she gave into the pain in her heart, sobbing loudly, in the secret confines of her bedroom. How could he do this to her?

***

Elder Ikpi was told by Joy's neighbours she had packed her things and left the compound a few days earlier. She did not leave a forwarding address.

He found her a couple of weeks later when the university reopened. He went to meet her in her department and insisted he had audience with her.

She indulged him after much persuasion.

He stared at her slim, pretty face, longingly, pleadingly. "Is this how you want to repay me, Joy?"

She snapped. "Please Chief, my name is Kokei. Stop calling me Joy."

"I—"

"I will repay you after my marriage. I already told my fiancé that you are domineering and manipulative…"

He slapped her. A resounding, shocking slap. Kokei's hand went to her face, and a tear dropped from her eyes unbidden. It was more from shock than pain. Elder Ikpi had never raised his hand to her before.

"Chief?"

"Over my dead body," Elder Ikpi said between his teeth.

"Don't be ridiculous. You never planned to marry me. You never even wanted me to have your child. Don't be silly, George. It's over between us."

She dared to use his first name, quickly wiping off the uncontrollable tears. She felt silly crying in front of him, despite the pain she still felt from the
resounding slap he had dealt her.

He looked into her eyes. "I will marry you, now if you want. Joy, I love you."

"Excuse me. I have a lecture now."

She side-stepped him before he could stop her and walked briskly toward a fast-filling lecture hall down the corridor.

"I will never let you go," he yelled after her.

CHAPTER-EIGHTEEN

Dodeye picked Kokei up in his Volvo after her lectures and noticed her dark mood. Her eyes were tainted red and one part of her face was swollen. As he drove out of the campus, he inquired.

"What's the matter, dearest?" he asked gently.

"My uncle was in my department today. Oh Dodeye, I wish he'll just let me be," she said, swallowing a sob.

Dodeye snapped. "What does he want?"

"I don't know. He threatened me, he even slapped me..."

"He did what?" Dodeye slammed the brake, reaching out to cup her face. "I think we should really bring in the police. See, my father is a friend of the Area Commander. You are not spending this your uncle's money anymore, why won't he leave you alone?"

Kokei sniffed. "I don't know."

"Is he just a distant uncle or what? Are you related? I don't understand..."

"I don't know either. My mother told me he is our uncle.

"The only relation she has anywhere in the world and that's it...I told him I was disowning him. I didn't get to know him anyway before I came to Calabar. Mom said he had always snubbed her because he was rich and we were not..."

"Anyway, you don't need him anymore. If he comes to harass you again, the police will pick him up." He smiled at her. "Cheer up, darling. It's alright."

"Where are you taking me?" she asked, trying to cheer up.

"A stage play. A colleague of mine won't stop disturbing me about so I agreed to come with you, today."

She chuckled. He laughed. "Hmn, sounds drab."

"Definitely will be. I'll take you for dinner afterwards," he said. "And then you know what will follow that." They both laughed.

The play was not drab at all. It was a rendition of the story of the prodigal son of the Bible, and Dodeye was so convicted after the altar call was made he dropped Kokei off immediately afterward, in the hostel accommodation she had secured as an alternative to Elder Ikpi's house.

Though he didn't surrender his life to Christ that night, it was a night of reflections. He had come a long way. His life and education had gone smoothly and his years in the London Business School and later at Harvard had placed him on a platform higher than most of his mates.

But at thirty-three, he was far from fulfilled. He ought to have been married. As he lay on his bed that night, he remembered the woman he was to have married. Kunbi. He had loved her more than his life. He had wanted to please her. He had thought she loved him too until she told him she was pregnant...for another man. A married man.

He remembered that night with pain. She had pleaded with him to forgive her. He had been so hurt but he loved her too much. He was ready to forgive her provided she terminated the pregnancy. And there lay the problem.

Kunbi had told him she just surrendered her life to Christ. After she discovered she was pregnant from the one-night mistake, she had wanted to commit suicide because she couldn't face the betrayal Dodeye would feel.

The hurt. The distrust. The pain.

She had over-dosed herself and it was only a miracle she survived with the foetus. The doctor had preached to her and she had surrendered her life.

No. She couldn't abort the child. She had wept that night. Ooh...Dodeye had never heard someone weep so much. She had clung to his feet as he made to leave. Leave forever. A job opportunity had just cropped up in Calabar. He had been invited to come and work as a Special Adviser to the State Governor on Policies and Economic Development. He had previously considered rejecting the offer. His successful businesses were in Lagos. His Kunbi was in Lagos. They had fixed their wedding date and would have even married earlier if not for the fact that he had to travel a lot.

Dodeye had taken the first flight the following day out of Lagos to Calabar to take up the appointment in his home state. He had chosen the easier way. The way of unforgiveness. He couldn't accept Kunbi's new faith, or the bastard child in her body.

He later heard Kunbi delivered a crippled baby. The drug overdose had done some damage on the
foetus.

He kept thinking she should have just aborted and moved on with him.

Dodeye clung to his pillow as he thought over his life.

He had never forgiven Kunbi. He wished he could. He really wished he could. He knew she wasn't yet married. He wanted her back especially now he had found the same conviction. He wished... wished... wished...

Dodeye did surrender his life to God the following Sunday when he attended his colleague's church. Kokei followed him to the altar, more for support than for the conviction. They were both followed up and gradually, Kokei got convicted too.

Dodeye's faith was so strong and firm he told her they had to break up and pray properly to be sure it was God's will for them to marry each other.

Kokei spent those days praying like never before. She loved Dodeye so much she thought she would die if she lost him now. And he was such a successful man. So handsome and so nice. She couldn't even begin to tell him the half of what she had done in her life for fear of losing him.

When Dodeye came back to her about a month after their separation to propose marriage, she was elated. The one month had been hell for her. She was on the verge of finding another man for herself when he came back. Saved!

Dodeye and Kokei got married in the heat of April, 1996. The wedding ceremony was a society one. Being a government official, and a good one too, the governor of the state and his beautiful wife were in attendance. Kokei's heart fluttered during the church service for fear Elder Ikpi would play pranks but little did she know she had nothing to fear.

Elder Ikpi was far from the wedding ceremony. He did not even hear about the much publicised occasion. A bank he took a loan from had demanded he vacate his house. He had taken the loan to pay for the house he bought in Ugep for Kokei, mortgaging the compound which housed his family.

When he took ill suddenly, he was forced to retire, and he had to sell the one-bedroom properties he owned. His financial situation had been so pitiable his wife and children had to move

to his father-in-law, Obol Otoma Ofem's house in Ugep. He had nothing left.

On the day of Kokei's wedding, Elder Ikpi was in the hospital. He suffered a major stroke, and died a few weeks later while she was still enjoying her honeymoon.

CHAPTER-NINETEEN

S*eptember 2008, Calabar*

Dodeye served the guests with non-alcoholic wine and freshly baked cake from his cook's special collection.

Obandi curled up on a single couch, hugged a huge teddy bear. Her pretty face was bare of makeup but her soft features remained attractive. She had just recovered from three months of morning sicknesses during which period she had stayed put in bed.

Dodeye's insistence she move to his house in Calabar had scared her beyond anything she had ever feared. To live in the same house with Kokei had been her greatest fear. She didn't love Dodeye. But she cared about nursing her mother's hurts against Kokei.

She had been fully aware of what she was going into. A loveless marriage, playing second fiddle to a confident woman. She had never imagined though, that Dodeye would show her any affection. Never imagined he would want her to live with him and his first family.

And when he did bring up the issue, she had not believed Kokei and her children would let her be.

"Obandi." Dodeye nudged her foot and she jerked out of her wandering thoughts. "I asked if you'll take some wine and cake," he said.

He leaned over her, his designer perfume choking her. To think she had been crazy about his Hugo Boss perfume before she got pregnant now seemed ridiculous. A few weeks earlier, she would feel nausea if he as much as entered the same room with her.

"I might try," she whispered.

He lifted himself off but she pulled him back with his shirt. When he looked at her, there was concern on his face.

"Must I be present in this meeting?" she said.

She breathed through her nose in the extent of her trepidation. She didn't want to sit through this confrontation. This coup d'état.

"I need you," he said simply, and patting her cheek, left her to bring her refreshments. She felt so young and fragile at just eighteen.

A student in the University of Calabar but so innocent. He had found her a virgin.

He'd told her he cherished this, and the only other woman he had had as a virgin was Kunbi, his first love. Old story.

Kunbi had never married anyone. He was doing all the marrying for the two of them. He had never gotten her out of his mind, and her crippled son. Her whole life was poured into the boy. What a way to live.

He served Obandi a slice of cake and the red wine, and gave her a peck on her forehead. Perhaps, one day, he would be able to love her as a woman and not a little sister.

"You'll be fine," he whispered.

She nodded, knowing she didn't believe him. She was scared to her bones. Dodeye had told her she must be in the meeting he summoned. After the shameful way she seduced him to get pregnant, she now stayed away as though he carried a plague. He had told her he knew she must have been encouraged by her revengeful mother.

***

Kokei entered her guest parlour, unaware a meeting had been conveyed.

She had been like a tenant in the house; not

seen her husband or his new wife, or aware of anything in her own home. Dodeye had hired the services of a cook so she had nothing to do with him.

Now he had people in their home and even asked them to use her private parlour. Next to her bedroom. The former master bedroom. Obandi had never been in this parlour but Kokei noticed she curled snugly on a single couch. Nneoyi and her father sat on the double couch. Pastor and Mrs. Bassey sat on the second double couch.

Dodeye sat on the other single couch opposite Obandi. There was no seat left for her.

She drew in a deep breath. "Good day. Pastor, Sis. Atai, welcome." She turned to leave but Dodeye's voice halted her.

"We are waiting for you," he said. This was the first time he would say more than a word to her in almost a year. She gazed at him as though a complete stranger.

"I'll be a minute." She excused herself.

The weather was cool due to rain fallen earlier on in the morning, and the air-conditioning in the house was chilling but Kokei sweated.

She walked as calmly as she could into her room and closed the door behind her. She felt choked suddenly. She could only imagine what was about to happen.

Dodeye had set her up. How he must hate her so. She knelt by her bed and prayed for God to help her.

She knew she had been unfaithful in the past but she had tried to clean up her act in the last twelve years. She changed out of the soft, silken kaftan she had worn into a simple cotton frock. She powdered her face and took a deep breath. Now was time to face the past.

She returned to the guest parlour where Dodeye had vacated the single couch for her. He was sprawled on the thick carpeted floor, leaning on Obandi's armrest.

"Take your seat," he said simply, and as she sat down, Pastor Bassey said a short prayer to open the meeting.

"I want to thank everyone for indulging me by coming for this impromptu meeting.

"I want to apologise to my wife for shocking her as well," Dodeye said. "I am forty-six years old. I have three lovely children, one more on the way.

"I am still a Christian, even though I agree I have compromised in certain areas.

He paused for a second. "I have achieved a lot in the business world. I am the proud owner of a chain of businesses like the Calabar Business School, which is already getting international acclaim, and a host of other business successes. I am a consultant to the Federal Government on Economic and Business related matters and recently I was installed the Obol Nkpeli of Ugep, howbeit very unceremoniously.

"Even my wife and children were not aware. I have had a tail of woes also. Recently, I impregnated a girl almost the age of my first son. Before I got married twelve years ago, I had jilted a host of women, thank God none of them had children for me." He sighed. "I have been a disappointment to my pastor, and the church, despite the fact that I am an alumnus of the Bible College.

"I have been a disappointment to my wife and kids as a husband and father. I have sought to be one tree that will make a forest and have failed.

"Today, my brief history is laid bare. Before
these witnesses, dear wife, Kokei, I want you to say
a brief history of your life." He looked at her, his eyes were so cold he could turn her to ice.

Strength left her bones. She'd been wondering where his long story was leading to. "What do you want, Dodeye? What is all this about?"

"What all this is about is you, and these people!" He waved at Nneoyi and the Obol Otoma. "They set me up to punish you. They used this foolish, innocent girl to hurt you. They have not only hurt her, they have hurt me, hurt themselves, and I daresay, hurt you that is if you have any flesh in your heart." His voice rose to a pitch. "You'll tell me, baby. You'll tell me right now why they hate you. Why they want to hurt you."

He flung himself to his feet. Obandi, gave a yelp and hugged her legs to herself.

CHAPTER-TWENTY

"If you want a history of my life, I'll tell you, when we are alone." Kokei gripped the arms of the couch, and her voice shook as she spoke. "Not here in the presence of everyone."

He clenched his fist. "Wife, I bet you, you'll tell me everything or else, you'll be shocked what I'll do to you."

"I don't care what you want to do—"

Nneoyi cut in. "I'll tell you what she did."

"Let them sort themselves," Obol Otoma Ofem said softly.

Kokei pressed her lips together. "You've had such a straight life and I don't. I'm sorry but my life cannot be summarised as easily as yours. Whatever you want to know, you will hear when we are alone."

"There won't be that opportunity. I am going to act as uncivil as you have pushed me to. You are going to vacate my premises right now. You will take your children with you, because I'm not even sure of their paternity..."

Atai moved swiftly to kneel before Kokei.

"Please tell him whatever he wants to hear. Put an end to all this problem in your life," Atai said. "Aren't you tired of the all this secrecy between you two? Will you rather he throws you out?"

"I am through with this marriage. May God forgive my wrong" Dodeye moved toward the entrance of the parlour.

Kokei jumped to her feet. "You cannot send me away! Where do I go to?"

"Dodeye," Pastor Bassey called, "come back here. Don't walk out on us."

Dodeye turned to look at him. "What is her relationship with Elder Nneoyi Ikpi?" Dodeye looked at Kokei.

Atai gestured her to answer from her kneeling position.

"I...ur... don't have..."

Dodeye growled. "The truth! Say it, Kokei!"

"I had a relationship with her husband." Kokei said. A soft gasp escaped Atai. She looked to her husband who was just as shocked. "But that was long ago. I never had any other man after you. I never cheated as a married woman," she said heatedly.

"How many men did you have before me?"

"I can't remember!"

"In fact, you were a professional whore before you met me!"

Kokei swallowed. "Am I on trial here?"

Pastor Bassey snapped. "Please just answer his questions so that we can all resolve this matter."

"I was dating only Elder Ikpi when I met you." Kokei bit out. They had no right to do this to her.

"Tell us about the relationship." Dodeye shoved his hands in his pocket and paced the small exquisite parlour. "How long did it last? Did you ever meet Mrs. Ikpi? Did her husband give you anything?"

"The relationship lasted almost four years." Kokei sighed. "I met Mrs. Ikpi once, her daughter was just about three years old. I slept in their house once but she just put to bed then and I didn't see her. He bought me a lot of things, I cannot recount them now." She cried.

"He bought you a Volkswagen. Did a very elaborate burial for your mother, emptied his savings account in the process.

"By the way, Obandi is a twin. I lost the second

one from a motorcycle account shortly after he bought you that car." Nneoyi swallowed hard.

"He made me believe he couldn't afford a second car and he was never there to take me and the babies out."

Atai gasped, Kokei shrunk back. Obandi hissed. Obol Otoma Ofem shook his head, and, Dodeye glared at Kokei.

Kokei exclaimed. "How was I supposed to know that? I never told him not to care for you."

Dodeye shouted. "You knew he was a married man!"

"That's not all he gave her. He sold properties in the home, deprived us of conveniences, luxuries, holidays just to please her. The four flats we built together with a loan was managed by her. She even stayed in one. We had to sell off that property to settle debts here and there." Nneoyi's voice scratched every surface in the room. "To cap it all up, he bought a property for her in Ugep. He mortgaged our house to buy her property. The bank took over our house when the loan matured. That's when he took ill. From ulcer to diabetes to cancer."

Pastor Bassey gaped. "Why didn't you stop him while he was doing all these?"

"I never knew a thing. The night she slept in our house, he told me she was a distant relative in transit. I had just had the twins and was still too weak to receive guests. They left the following morning. I had always been a housewife. He never wanted me to work. He was a very loving husband while at home and a possessive one too. He lied to me all the while, and I believed him. He lied he was travelling for a conference in Port-Harcourt. The conference was actually holding but he went to the Obudu Cattle Ranch with her..."

"How did you find all these out?" Atai whispered, with were tears in her eyes.

"On his deathbed, he told me everything. He begged me to forgive him. She just dumped him shamelessly. By the time he died, he had nothing left. No property, on money, no hope," Nneoyi said. "I moved with my children to my father's house in the village. He even had no house in the village. He had told me he bought a land but there were no papers. I trusted him too much. He betrayed me." If she sobbed, it would have been preferred to the raw emotions in her hoarse voice.

Dodeye leaned on the wall, as though afraid he would slump. He had jilted Kunbi, repentant, loving Kunbi to marry a devil-incarnate. How had this Kokei won his heart so easily?

Kokei leaned back. "I didn't know all this. I'm sorry. I didn't..."

Dodeye yelled. "Shut your mouth."

"That's why I made up my mind. I decided to revenge. And that's why I also came to tell you about her. I told myself every day since the day my husband died that I will follow her up and I did that judiciously. She was a wicked husband-snatcher...I was ready to go to any lengths to hurt her back..."

Dodeye fixed his gaze on Kokei. "Come to think of it. That uncle of yours, what was his name? I never asked."

"He wasn't an uncle, okay. He was Elder Ikpi, her husband." Kokei slid to her knees. "Dodeye, I am sorry."

"How can I ever forgive you? How could I have prayed and entangled myself with a wretch like this? How am I sure you're not lying even now. That the children you call mine are really mine?" Dodeye heaved.

"Dodeye please, please. I never cheated on you. I swear." Kokei held his ankle. "I cleaned up my act. Please forgive me!"

"You lied about your family. You lied about the kind of person you are. In fact, you live a lie. I don't know how you could have manipulated a married man to his death. You manipulated me to marry you. You must have used some evil powers..."

Kokei shook her head frantically. "No, no, no."

"It was just luck. Please forgive me. Mrs. Ikpi forgive me. Please. Obandi. Pastor help me beg them. Help me beg him..." She crawled to Pastor Bassey, wailing.

"Listen to me. That house in Ugep, you are handing it over to Mrs. Ikpi..."

"We don't want anything from her," Obol Otoma Ofem interjected.

"I insist. The other properties in town here, I am going to buy them back myself. You have the right to your husband's property," Dodeye said.

"It is not necessary," Nneoyi answered.

"Ask your first son to see me tomorrow unfailingly."

"We will not take anything from you..."

"You'll take this one. Obandi," Dodeye looked at the sullen teenager. "I am sorry I touched you at all. That child in your womb is my full responsibility and after that, you are free to remarry, to become the woman you want. I will never joke with anything that concerns you or your future, your family. I am indebted. As for you..." he turned fully to look at Kokei and remembered the day he walked out on Kunbi. His heart lurched. He would do it again. He would give the unfaithful her due.

"As for you," he stammered. "I have nothing more to do with you."

THE END

Every man gets the wife he deserves.
Bishop Tunde Adeleye.

TEASER FROM THE AUTHOR

ALTERNATE TITLES: Discuss why any of these titles may be more appropriate.

1. WAY OF THE UNFORGIVING.
2. WAY OF THE UNFORGETFUL.
3. WAY OF THE REVENGEFUL.

CHOOSE A TITLE OF YOUR OWN AND GIVE REASONS FOR IT.

Acknowledgments

Brother Michael Inah and Sister Monica Ikpi
Dr. Inah Okon, and Ifeoluwa Ogunyinka

THE NIGERIAN CHILD – MY VISION

Hab. 2:2 Then the LORD answered me and said: "Write the vision And make it plain on tablets, That he may run who reads it.

More than before, it's time for the well-to-do to cater for the less-privileged. Over the past few years, the Lord has laid this burden for THE NIGERIAN CHILD on my heart and I believe it's time to spread the vision. I have a desire to help and to instigate help for THE NIGERIAN CHILD. There are currently five areas of help I have been able to identify.

1.   THE MARKET-SCHOOL PROJECT: this vision is aimed at eradicating street and market hawking in the long run. The strategy is to erect schools in market places where children hawking can take a few hours out to learn and then go back to their jobs. It is a long term project and a highly capital intensive one.

2.   THE BREAD AND MILK PROJECT: bread and milk will be given in the morning time to children trekking to school just before school resumes. It can be done once a month, once a week or every day. Or as rampantly as the provision is available. It is not very capital intensive and as little as N50 or $0.35 (US dollar) can feed a child with bread and warm milk

3.   THE UMBRELLA PROJECT: to help alleviate

the suffering of children who hawk on the streets (while we work towards eradicating hawking on our streets), by providing umbrellas especially during the rainy season. The umbrellas can also be useful during the scotching hot weathers. Umbrellas of different sizes will be given depending on the size of the child. Prices of umbrellas range from N350.00 to N500.00 or $2.50 to $3.50 (US dollar).

4.   THE SORT-A-CHILD PROJECT: which is aimed at helping at least a child in whatever capacity you can. It can be by paying a sick child's hospital bills, buying food and clothing for a child or paying a child's school fees. It can be as long as a life-time commitment or a one-time affair.

5.   THE STUDENT CARE PROJECT: for secondary and tertiary students who can't afford their

school fees. The idea is to help through the bob-a-job initiative.

THE NIGERIAN CHILD vision is not another non-governmental, money-spinning organisation. It is service to God and provision for THE NIGERIAN CHILD. It can be done privately or corporately. The important thing is to help a NIGERIAN CHILD.

I beg to challenge EVERY CHURCH IN NIGE-RIA to adopt the SORT-A-CHILD PROJECT or as the Lord lay it on our hearts.

HELP!
Signed - *THE NIGERIAN CHILD*

TRUE DREAM SERIES:
COMPLIMENTARY NIGHT
BOSS LADY
DUMPED
YOUR WISH IS MINE
EVEN THE LAWFUL CAPTIVE
HE TAKETH THE FIRST
THE OTHER SISTER
WHAT'S GOOD FOR THE GOOSE
SERVE A KOBO
JUST LIKE PLAY
SHATTERED
SCATTERED
IYKE'S REVENGE
ÌKA
BATTERED
BASIS FOR LOVE

NOVELS:

TO WHERE THE WIND BLEW (BOOK 1, EIBA
FAMILY SAGA)

SCENT OF WATER

PEPPER

FRAIL FLESH

THE DAYS AFTER THAT NIGHT

TISHA

EIBA FAMILY SAGA:

TO WHERE THE WIND BLEW

PROMISE TOMORROW